Belle and Sébastien

The Child of the Mountains

Belle
and
Sébastien

The Child of the Mountains

Cécile Aubry

Translated by Gregory Norminton

Illustrations by Helen Stephens

ALMA CLASSICS

ALMA CLASSICS
an imprint of

ALMA BOOKS LTD
3 Castle Yard
Richmond
Surrey TW10 6TF
United Kingdom
www.almaclassics.com

Belle and Sébastien first published in French as *Belle et Sébastien –
L'Enfant de la montagne* in 1965
First published in hardback by Alma Classics in 2016
This new paperback edition first published in 2018

Text © Hachette Livre, 2014
Cover image and text illustrations © Helen Stephens, 2016

Translation © Gregory Norminton, 2016

Extra Material © Alma Classics

This book is supported by the Institut Français (Royaume-Uni) as part
of the Burgess programme

Printed in Great Britain by CPI Group (UK) Ltd, Croydon CR0 4YY

ISBN: 978-1-84749-725-3

TO MY SON

1

When the woman had walked through Saint Martin, no one had paid her the slightest attention. Who could have imagined that she was going up there, towards the pass, in her wide gypsy skirts, her worn flat shoes, and protected only by the shawl that covered her from head to hip? Freezing rain had been falling since dawn. Those villagers with reasons to be outside walked briskly with heads bowed: there was nothing to see in such foul January weather. They looked at nothing.

Towards midday, the wind changed direction, bringing snow. At the edge of the village, the woman had taken the short cut that leads to the border and the Baou refuge. Had she taken the usual route, she would have gone past old César's house, and

Angelina would have noticed her. Surprised, moved at the sight of her walking on her own towards the Baou and so poorly protected against the cold, she would have spoken to her. Perhaps she would have persuaded her to settle down drowsily in the warmth of the fire, to wait for better weather instead of setting off into the storm – she and the child she was carrying, so close to being born. However, the woman was going up by the short cut. And so that silent enemy, the snow, took her, hugging her closely in its merciless softness.

She was going on her way, sinking with each step, buffeted by swirling snow, using up her strength. What was her destination? No one ever found out. Several times, she fell, and then picked herself up. Near the dry stone refuge, at the foot of the Baou, she fell for the last time – a little black speck in that immense whiteness.

It was the hour at which Johannot and Berg, the customs men, were coming back from their patrol. The routine of their work had brought them together without erasing their differences. Berg was short, thin, with a narrow face and pale, watery eyes. His aggressiveness had no effect on tall, calm Johannot, his elder.

"It's a crying shame to send men out on patrol in such weather! You can't see ten metres in front of you!"

Johannot shrugged his shoulders in resignation.

"It's our job," he said.

He spoke little and preferred to use short sentences that said only what he meant. He pointed his chin towards the shadow that was coming towards them through the frenzy of icy flakes.

"Looks like César over there."

The shadow took on more substance.

"Hey, César!" cried Johannot. Then he added, irrefutably, "filthy weather!"

César, as they met, paused a moment to chat: he had few friends, but Johannot was one of them.

"Good for foxes, mind," he said.

The white bristles on his cheeks showed that he was an old man, but he gave such an impression of endurance, with such a blend, in his gaze, of meditative depth and audacity, that it was difficult to guess his age. He seemed barely to be into his fifties, whereas in fact he had just passed sixty.

"Good hunting as ever?" asked Berg, nodding at the old man's rifle.

"Oh," replied César, "today I'm just going for a stroll."

Berg glanced in disgust at the great white expanse and the pristine snow plummeting from a dismal grey sky. "Suit yourself," he said, as if to say, "to hell with you, you old lunatic – you and your passion for the mountains in all seasons." He started to walk again and added, "We're heading back to the station this minute!"

César tapped a finger to his fur hat: "Good day."

Johannot returned his farewell: "My regards to Angelina and Jean…"

With Berg ahead of him, he resumed the arduous hike, heading up towards the Baou refuge, which they had to get round in order to reach the customs post. César, meanwhile, took off towards the valley.

Johannot was the first to notice the black speck as he and Berg were approaching the refuge.

"Berg, what is that… over there?"

Berg was walking with his head bowed against the icy bite of the snow, warming himself with thoughts of the hot stove that awaited them…

"What?" he said.

Already Johannot was veering towards the figure, on which the snow was piling up.

"It looks like a body," he groaned, trying with all his might to run through the soft snow.

Berg followed more slowly. He saw Johannot kneel, clear the snow from a face and turn to call down the slope:

"César! Hey, César!"

Berg, in turn, tried to run.

At the sound of Johannot's cries, César had turned around. He could no longer see the two customs men, but their anxious calls made him retrace his steps. Soon he was able to distinguish the two of them, grey shadows in the whiteness, bent over a figure. He quickened his wide, slow gait and saw, at that moment, the woman whose head Johannot was lifting as he attempted to get a few drops from his flask past her lips. The poor wretch opened her eyes. César knelt down.

"We have to carry her down to the village," Johannot said. "You'll help us, César."

"How did she get up here," Berg muttered, "in this weather and in her condition?"

Johannot shrugged. He asked himself no questions – he knew only that they had to get her down to the village, to Doctor Guillaume, and that it would be no easy task in the blizzard and given her condition.

"Hurry," he said. "Let's go."

"She looks like a gypsy," said Berg. "There was a camp of them in the valley last month."

The woman whimpered softly. Johannot stroked her brow and, in his helplessness, said repeatedly:

"There, there, love. It's all right, we're here."

He stood up and gave instructions:

"Berg, you take her feet. César, you and I take her shoulders. Let's try to go quickly and not jolt her."

However, César looked up at him:

"There isn't time. When a ewe has this woman's look, the shepherd stays with her..."

He jerked his chin towards the refuge:

"That's where we have to take her. The village is too far."

They did as César had suggested, Berg at her feet, César and Johannot at her shoulders. Their laborious progress dragged groans out of the unconscious woman. Her shawl had fallen and her long brown hair swept the snow. They settled her on the earthen floor of the refuge. At least she was sheltered from the wind. They could see now how young she was, and pity clutched at the hearts of the three men.

César took off his sheepskin jacket and slipped it under the woman's body.

"Stay with her, César," Johannot said. "Berg and I are going down to fetch the doctor."

They had gone already, snatched up by the snow-fog, when César called them back.

"Tell my granddaughter, Angelina, on your way... she's young, but she'll be able to help Guillaume better than us. Tell them to bring up everything necessary for the mother... and for the little one."

He had spoken those last words in a lower voice, a voice charged with meaning, as if already, even before Sébastien had come into the world, he was assuming full responsibility, not on a surge of emotion, but deep in his conscience. His thoughtful gaze followed Berg and Johannot as they resumed their journey to the valley. They soon fell out of sight, and he returned to the refuge. The snow had almost stopped, but the wind was blowing fiercely. All around the shelter, the battle raged between the mountain and the elements, the same battle since the dawn of time: wind against stone, amid a terrible howling.

Inside the refuge, another drama was playing itself out: one that César could only watch powerlessly. Even as death was snatching the woman away, she was giving birth to new life. Once again in this old world, the great mystery followed its course: a little child gave its first cry of despair. The old man, who had helped deliver so many lambs, repeated actions that were familiar to him. Then he took the jacket, which was no longer of use to the mother, and wrapped the child in the woollen fleece.

When the others got back from the village, they saw César at the entrance to the refuge with something in his arms. The wind had eased off and the great silence of the snow spread across the mountain; voices carried a long way, and they heard the raging cries of the newborn. Angelina's fourteen years made her light-footed. She arrived first. The doctor was young and he was close behind her.

"You're too late, Guillaume," César told him. "But it can't be helped."

"We came as fast as we could, César."

Johannot arrived next, followed by Berg and little Jean, who, being ten, saw in this dramatic episode nothing more than an opportunity to race up the mountain. Everybody stood still as the doctor came out of the refuge. Pity and solemnity blended in his youthful face.

"It's over..." he said. "That child is alone in the world."

Angelina looked at her grandfather, the prayer of a woman in her young girl's eyes. Therefore, he held out the child to her.

"He's the son of the mountain. I know that you will love him – you and your brother Jean."

The newborn had fallen asleep in the warm lamb's wool. Angelina wrapped him up in her shawl and quickly turned towards the valley... Something like terror surged up in her before the frozen whiteness of the high peaks, whose shadows reached menacingly as far as her feet as she held the child. She had only one thought: to get away. Get away to the human warmth of the hearth in the tall fireplace, which she had covered with embers before setting out, and there to set down the fragile little life that had so miraculously been saved.

"Go with them, Guillaume," César said simply. "There's nothing more for you to do here."

Johannot added:

"We'll do what needs to be done for the mother, Doctor... Besides, these little ones are so delicate. He at least has to make it!"

Jean was already running towards the house. He stopped:

"What about his name?... He doesn't have a name!"

César, who was about to go back into the refuge, halted.

"Today," he said, "is St Sebastian's day..."

Angelina looked up at the doctor:

"Sébastien?" she asked.

He returned her smile. Then, gently, she hugged the formless heap in her arms.

"Come to our house, Sébastien... We will love you... Oh, how we'll love you."

Far below, the smoke from chimney fires lit for the evening meal climbed into the icy air above the village. Angelina, Guillaume and Jean hurried towards that light-blue mist, and it was as if, suddenly, the world had become young again.

On that same day, 20th January, the feast day of St Sebastian, while a child came into the world amid the stormy heights, Belle was born at the opposite end of the mountain chain, much farther down in the valley.

This was at Pasco's farm. Bernadette, the elder of the daughters, was carefully entering the date in her homework book when her sister, Christine, ran up to her.

"Come and see! The puppies are born! Leave your homework: come quickly!"

There was no need to hurry her. Bernadette had pulled her shawl off the coat rack, and was running to the stable where they kept the large bitch locked up. She was a huge beast, with silky fur, who had on her majestic person only three markings: her nose and her two eyes – two eyes whose golden pupils were veiled by long black lashes.

Bernadette, with Christine in tow, pushed the door open. The large dog lifted her head. Having recognized her visitors, she bent towards the squirming, damp little things and licked them passionately.

"Oh!" said Bernadette, full of disappointment, "They'll never be as beautiful as her. In fact, they're hideous."

"That's not true," explained Christine. "They're superb. You don't know anything."

Their father arrived.

"Daddy," said Christine, "Bernadette thinks they're ugly."

"Of course they're ugly. But just you wait a few days and you'll see what beautiful white furballs you have."

With this assurance, they closed the door, leaving the bitch and her little ones in peace. Bernadette returned to her homework and Christine to her games.

The next day saw the visit of Gédéon, the pedlar, who was in the habit of calling at the farm twice a year. Pasco saw him coming up the stony track, his wheezy car, which belonged to another age, straining against the slope.

"Gédéon!" Pasco called. "You were after a big dog to keep you company on your travels… I've got a litter, born yesterday."

Gédéon stopped the jolting and squeaking machine that he called his car in the farmyard.

"Let's take a look," he said.

In the stable, he considered the three pups, picked one up, weighed it in his hand, scrutinized its little pink-and-black muzzle, its ears and big clumsy paws, all under the baleful stare of its mother.

"Easy girl, calm down," he said as he laid the puppy between her paws. He turned to Pasco: "Fine animals, I'll grant you. But this one's the best-looking…"

He pointed at the one he had just examined:

"Are you giving her to me, Pasco?"

Faced with the farmer's prudent silence, he added:

"In exchange, you can choose a watch for yourself and two more for your daughters… not forgetting a silk scarf for your wife, of course."

As he spoke, he went back to the car and returned, carrying a large box. He took out a selection of watches, whose casings he opened, and a handful of silk scarves printed in lively colours…

"Put that away," said Pasco, "and in three months' time, when you come to collect your dog, you'll give us what you owe us."

And so it was that Belle was sold for three watches and a silk scarf. It was the first time in her life, but it would not be the last. For if there is variety in human destiny, the same is true for dogs.

CHAPTER I

Belle was entirely happy with the pedlar. He was
proud of her. Even when she was still a puppy,
you could tell what she would become: huge and
strong like her mother, tender and gentle at the
offer of friendship, menacing when angered. She
was admired and loved or feared by all. When she
turned about with her slow and steady gait, the
way she carried her head astounded people. You
could glimpse the powerful beauty, the assurance
and the pride of a wild beast that she would one
day possess. A connoisseur, who would have liked
to buy her off Gédéon, told him that he would have
to be wary of that strength.

"Nonsense! She's as gentle as a lamb."

"Just you wait until she's grown and you'll see."

"Madam," Gédéon replied, "she's not a creature
you'd want to annoy! I'm quite happy for folk to
be a bit scared of her..."

And so Belle reached the age of five months.

One day, Gédéon's hiccupping, rattling, wheez-
ing car stopped in town, blocking a private drive.
Gédéon got out and Belle followed him. A driver
in his van shouted at the pedlar:

"What about me, then? How am I going to get in?"

Gédéon was hot-tempered:

"It's the only space and I won't be a minute!"

"Oh yes! I've heard that one before! Only I don't
have time to waste – I'm working!"

Gédéon went up to him, hostility on his face:

"How about me? What do you think I'm doing here? I've just got a parcel to deliver and I'll be right back."

"Like I care! Take your old banger elsewhere, or I'll do it for you."

"Just you try!"

Belle, sniffing here and there, wandered off to explore the world. She heard Gédéon's voice once more, calling God as witness to his woes.

"Damn it all! Find somewhere else to park! Preventing honest folk from earning a living!"

The door slammed and Gédéon, distracted by his rage, started his engine. The young dog trotted towards the familiar sound. She ran behind the car... and lost sight of it. So she ran on and on, straight ahead, without knowing where or why.

By the time Gédéon realized that he had forgotten her, it was too late. He searched long and hard for her, but never saw her again.

Belle galloped for ages – as long as her strength held out. Finally, in despair, she sat down and whimpered. She happened to do this in the very middle of the main road, and so it was that she met Roger Pouillou.

He was a lorry driver and he was heading back to Lyon. The weather had turned foggy. Roger, cautious by nature, had put his floodlights on. When Belle saw those two monstrous great eyes coming towards her, she stood up, expecting an attack.

Roger Pouillou was a strong man, but tender-hearted, friendly with animals and easily unsettled. Frantically he blew his horn and flashed his lights. It was no use. There stood Belle, sure of her rights, determined to hold her ground. Faced with this immovable animal, Roger braked. The dog wore a collar; Gédéon's knife had etched into it the single name: BELLE. It was not much to go on! Confronted with this problem, Roger took off his cap, put it on again and, scratching the crown of his head relentlessly, explained to the dog:

"You certainly are Belle! But you're lost. Not even your master's name… Nothing! So what am I going to do with you? It's not safe, you know, to be strolling about the roads. Didn't you know that?"

The dog looked at him with eyes of molten gold, a trembling tail and friendly whimpers. It was more than enough to win Roger over. He took Belle into his arms and installed her next to him on the seat.

"Blimey! You're not light, that's for sure."

Belle, comfortably rolled up into a ball, gave Roger the tenderest of looks. The big lorry started up.

Roger Pouillou got out at the first gendarmerie. The gendarmes he spoke to looked at the bitch:

no, there were no dogs of this breed in the area. No, they were not set up for deliveries of this sort.

"Especially," said one of the gendarmes facetiously, "considering that in three months' time, this animal will come up to your waist."

Roger Pouillou was six feet tall; he looked at Belle and gave an admiring whistle.

"Even so, we can't just leave her wandering about."

The gendarme suggested that there was always the Society for the Protection of Animals.

"Alternatively," said his colleague, "leave us your name and address and take her with you. If in a year and a day no one's come looking for her, she's yours!"

Roger Pouillou gestured at the distance between his elbow and the floor. The gendarme shrugged a shoulder in resignation: really, there was nothing he could do.

Roger signed a form and took Belle with him. He warned her:

"I wonder how Juliette is going to take to you."

In the event, Juliette took to her very well. She adored her husband and his presents. It little mattered that their lodgings consisted of one small bedroom and a doll's-house kitchen: she welcomed Belle as a gift from Heaven.

And Belle lived very happily at the home of her third owner. She spent eight months there, and grew to full size. It was at this point that the caretaker of the apartment building made up her mind to intervene.

One day, Roger came back from his travels to find Juliette in tears. Belle, huge and magnificent, took up the entire room, while the caretaker, who was trying to be comforting even as she failed to sympathize, dabbed with her handkerchief at Juliette's blue eyes, as if she were four years old.

"Come, come, Madame Pouillou," she said. "There, there, dear! There's no point getting so upset! You know very well, I've been trying to keep the tenants happy for all the months you've had that animal. I've always told them, 'At least wait until someone comes to claim her! Surely, someone has to come and fetch her some day!'"

Roger glanced solemnly at Belle, and then even more sadly at Juliette.

"Yes," he said, "but no one has come."

Juliette gave a start: "Just as well!"

This reaction made the caretaker more severe:

"And there it is, my dearest! Only the management agent is always telling me, 'Madame Martin, no animals in the building!' So you know… if it had only been a little dog, who's to say? But a beast like that! I can't very well pretend not to notice her, can I?"

Roger acted tenderly. He even tried putting on the face that usually made Juliette laugh. It was no use. She merely shrugged her shoulders and sobbed more loudly.

"You're all brutes… heartless!"

This injured Roger to his core:

"You're going too far, Juliette. I've been bending over backwards for months so you could keep that dog… But you have to face facts: she's no trinket!"

For the caretaker, who was a woman of common sense, the only task left was to pronounce her decision. Having done so, she left. Juliette acknowledged this departure with a furious sniff, and fell into contemplation of Belle. This only deepened her despair, so Roger confessed to an idea that he had been keeping secret for some time:

"How about we give her to my mate Guichard… I've spoken to him about it. He's game… and he's got a garden!"

Juliette's indignant cry told him that he was on the wrong track.

"No, no, *no*! I'd rather pack our bags and get out of here… Roger! Why don't we leave, the three of us?"

Roger, distraught, could only murmur:

"Juliette, sweet pea… where would we go?"

Juliette had no idea, and besides, what did she care? She had only one constant thought: Belle. What would become of her?

"You really love her that much," observed Roger. "It's unbelievable!"

All of a sudden, he felt a surge of anger:

"It's idiotic, it's childish! She's only a dog, after all! You wouldn't want to ruin both our lives for this animal, would you?"

No doubt it was this anger that made Juliette deploy her last line of defence. She said very quickly:

"We can go and stay with Mummy…"

At first, Roger was close to breaking something; then he turned cold and hard:

"All right, I get it. Pack your suitcases. Let's go and wind up at your mother's… A lovely treat for her, a fine mess for us! I'm going to get some air – goodnight."

The door slammed shut, and for all that Juliette called out, "Roger!" the only response from her husband was the diminishing sound of his footsteps hurrying down the stairs. Juliette looked at Belle with eyes full of tears: it was no longer a matter of childish sorrow – she knew now that the dog was lost to her. Those golden eyes watched her and Juliette answered them:

"It's the first time we've really argued, Roger and me."

In losing Juliette and Roger, Belle lost the happiness that she had known for almost a year. For her it was sudden, tragic and impossible to understand. She let herself be led, of course, to the "mate" Guichard, and there she waited... However, when neither Juliette nor Roger came, she ran away. She wandered famished for two days. Then, on the third morning...

A fairground was being set up in some suburb. A young man was crunching an apple while watching Belle as she wandered, ferreting about in search of something to eat. What a marvellous animal, he thought, and he smiled: he enjoyed watching her. All of a sudden, he tossed the apple away and his smile vanished: he was no longer looking at the dog but at a police car as it halted, slyly, with scarcely a sound. An officer stepped out. He carried in his hand one of those long, supple steel wires used to garrotte stray dogs. The pound! The youth took a few swift paces to place himself between the dog and the police officer.

"Hey! That dog's mine."

"Well then, you could try taking care of it. We've been informed that this animal has been wandering the neighbourhood since last night."

"That... I can't deny. We got here last night."

The officer had taken out his notebook.

"Name... address? It's against the law to let dogs roam the public highway..."

"My name is Mario. Can't give you an address – don't have one. I'm a juggler at the circus, over there... So, here one day, somewhere else the next... See what I mean?"

"Mario what?"

"Boulonni. That's my father's name. Mario Boulonni..."

Once more, Belle found herself among people. As soon as he had laid a hand on her, she loved Mario. He was a being full of grace. For hours at a time, she watched him throw the most unlikely things in the air and catch them again. Sometimes he surrounded himself with flaming sticks, and Belle growled. At other times, he brought to life long ribbons of silk that traced a supple and gaudy dance around him. Multicoloured balls fell back miraculously into his hands. Ladders as they held him up seemed to float in the air, and he performed a thousand improbable stunts with a half-smile, as if none of it required the least effort. Yes, he was a strange being, quite unlike other men, and Belle adored him.

She followed him from town to town and, each night, went on stage with him. There, in the twinkling of lights and in his sequinned costume, Mario pulled off his amazing feats. He was weightlessness itself. He juggled bubbles of air, stars.

One night, in a big city, when Mario's extravaganza was over and he had left the stage with Belle, a member of the audience asked to speak to Folco Boulonni, Mario's father. Then, after the show, when they had turned off the lights, Folco came to find his son.

"I've been offered an top-notch contract for you. You will start in England, then all of Europe... Naturally, you'll leave the dog here."

"No," said Mario.

"What? You'd turn down the chance to become *Mister* Mario Boulonni? To appear in the world's great circuses?"

"I will go wherever you want, but with her."

"Unbelievable! I must have dropped you on your head when you were little!"

Folco turned gentle and conciliatory:

"We'll look after her, she'll be happy here. When your contract is over, you'll come back... You'll see her again."

"It's no use going on about it. I'm happy here. I don't want a change."

Mario held out for a month. Then ambition, the longing for glory, that feeling like vertigo which takes hold of an artist when he steps out on stage to public applause, all of this did its work. Mario signed his contract. That very day he gave up on Belle, and Folco, after his son's departure, sold her. She had grown even bigger than her mother, and her fur, pampered like that of all circus animals, surrounded her with a snowy fleece – thick, long, as bright as a polar bear's, in which only the black stains of her nose and the long slits of her eyes showed. Her beauty was dazzling. Folco fetched a good price for her.

So began for Belle the itinerant life of a pedigree dog. Bought on a whim, sold, changing owner every time she became a nuisance or someone offered a lot of money for her, she became merchandise. People haggled over her as they might for an item of furniture. She changed hands, admired constantly for her exceptional beauty, but she learnt to distrust humans, who so easily give and then take away their friendship. She became indifferent. It mattered little to her where she was being taken, she did not give her heart away.

She was about six years old when she was locked up in a kennel. On the register, it said, "Belle, Pyrenean Mountain Dog." It took two men armed with forked sticks to push her into the cage on which were displayed the shameful words: "Aggressive dog". A word was added to the register – "Dangerous" – beside her name. For two days, she refused to eat. Then she calmed down and resumed that air of indifferent meekness that made one of her new masters say:

"She's a beauty, but she's not an intelligent beast."

People forgot to be wary of her. They did not know that, in the suffering of her imprisonment, the animal was rediscovering the cunning of her wild ancestors. Her keeper learnt this to his cost. One day when he opened the cage, the dog leapt out, without a bark, silent as a wolf. She struck the man mid-chest. He fell...

...And Belle, heeding the call of the high mountains where her breed originated, fled towards whatever refuge they might offer her.

2

In truth, Belle's escape, that leap which made her overcome centuries of domestication and gave her back the freedom of her wild ancestors, was only the trap in which she had to get herself caught in order to find Sébastien. "Nothing happens by chance, everything has meaning." Destiny was throwing its dice; Belle and Sébastien, the big dog and the little boy, were going to pick them up, play and win.

It all began one Saturday, market day in Saint-Martin. On the worksite of EDF, the sirens sounded midday, and the workers downed tools and headed towards the village in groups. One of these consisted of Gabriel, François and Jean, old César's grandson, who had just turned sixteen.

"Look out!" cried Gabriel.

He flung out his hand just in time to hold back Jean, who, turning to face François, had not seen a wooden barrel hurtling down the slope. It was a narrow escape. The barrel rolled over to the opposite bank, turned back on itself and came to a halt. Out of it, comically, a little boy emerged, declaring with a peal of laughter:

"I'm the barrel that rolls on its own!"

"Oh, very clever," grumbled Gabriel. "You could have broken a leg, not to mention your head, you little maniac!"

He walked on: let Jean tell the kid off. The little one's expression grew so intense that he looked affronted.

"Sébastien," cried Jean sternly. "I might have known it would be you!"

"Oh, no," Sébastien protested, "you knew nothing about it."

"If you were my lad," said a passing worker, "you'd get a hiding."

Sébastien, at six years of age, was strongly inclined to indiscipline and a lack of respect for grown-ups. He shrugged his shoulders.

"That's enough, Sébastien," said Jean.

The men, in chorus, added a few heartfelt and unsympathetic comments concerning the difficulties that must befall an honest family that adopts a child of unknown origin. They were not cruel men, but they spoke aloud what everyone in Saint-Martin thought. Sébastien gave them a dirty look, and then shrugged his shoulders with a kind of lordliness. Finally, the laughter returned to his face as he told Jean:

"The goat is in fine form."

"And you came here to tell me that?"

"No," Sébastien conceded. "Angelina is at the market. She says you have to come and help her load the mule."

Jean took the child's hand.

"What about my barrel?" Sébastien cried.

"We'll find you another."

Sébastien sensed complicity in this. He was careful not to smile, but he gave his hand to Jean. Leaving behind the men who were walking with steady steps along the loose stone track, they went running down to the village. There they headed towards Angelina's basket stall at the foot of the steps in front of the church.

Market day was ending; villagers were tidying away their empty crates and taking down their stalls. The weather was very mild for the time of year, and a fair number of men wasted their time strolling back and forth in front of Angelina's wickerwork, partly to look at her baskets... mostly for the pleasure of receiving a proud or amused glance, or a well-timed rejoinder.

Just now, she was gathering her merchandise in large and lightweight clusters and tying them to the mule's packsaddle. The pretty beast stood obediently, even as she glanced greedily through her long lashes at a crate of cabbages. We should not let a mule's placid expression fool us, for by dint of stretching her neck, Paquita achieved her goal. First one, then two of old Mathieu's cabbages were delicately munched. As the stout fellow stood up for his rights, Angelina sided with the mule: withered cabbages! The whole crate was unsellable and Mathieu knew it!

This provoked a response. All the saints honoured in Provence got dragged into the argument, and finally Mathieu declared himself ready to settle for a goat's cheese. At that price, Angelina demanded the whole crate. Paquita ate her fill, and all ended cheerfully under the dazzling light of the Provençal mountains that fine winter's morning.

Jean left Sébastien at the entrance to the square and went to see his sister. A group of boys had been waiting for this moment to surround Sébastien. Antoine, the gang leader, started:

"Hey, Sébastien! Still a gypsy?"

Suddenly the words boomed into a chant:

"Sé-bas-tien, gyp-sy boy... Sé-bas-tien, gyp-sy boy...!"

They formed a circle about him, and he forced his way through with blows of his fist, his head, but without speaking a word, his face hardened with rage and pride. A man carrying his wares almost dropped them and cried out:

"Go and fight somewhere else..." Then, calling the market as his witness: "Will you look at these little devils! Ah, it's a crying shame!"

He did not say whether the crying shame related to his having been jostled by brats, or to the pitilessness of these children who rounded as a group on someone who was different from them. When the man had gone, Antoine resumed:

"So, tell me, Sébastien, is your goat still poorly?"

There was an explosion of general hilarity, delighted cackles and knowing elbow jabs.

"Eh, did you hear that he went to fetch Doctor Guillaume to treat his goat?"

"Hey, dimwit! Don't you know what a vet is?"

"Do you give your goat compresses?"

"Do you put her to bed?"

From the first words, Sébastien had frozen. Unmoving, full of contempt, he stared them down one after the other, without responding to their sarcasm. Irritated by the pride, the hardness of this little lad who showed no fear of their numbers, they closed in on him, pushing ever more closely against him. So Sébastien charged, head down, like his goat.

"Get lost, I'm in a hurry."

The ranks gave way to this charge.

"Hey! Till next time, gypsy!"

Then came the parting shot:

"No need to be so uppity, kid!"

However, Sébastien had broken the circle and was running across the little square towards the church.

"You've been fighting again," said Angelina, looking severely at the state of Sébastien.

He turned and eyed the group of schoolboys keeping itself well out of cuffing range: Angelina had quick reflexes and a swift hand, and everybody knew it.

"Can't you hear them? They call me the gypsy! I don't like it."

"Just don't reply," said placid Jean.

"I didn't reply – I bashed into 'em."

Sébastien's satisfaction was obvious. Victorine, the village grocer, had left her trestles for a moment to go and choose a basket from Angelina's display.

"Jean's right," she declared, as she weighed one of the baskets. "It's all just childish teasing. They're daft, lad! Don't listen to them."

Angelina's tone sharpened:

"If you think the little one enjoys it!"

And, because she was ready to take on the whole world to defend Sébastien, he was the one she scolded:

"One day it'll take a turn for the worse, and then they'll hurt you!… Here, go and buy me a pack of buttons, some needles and white thread."

Sébastien widened his eyes until they were as big as gemstones.

"All that?"

"Yes, all that! Look, I'll write it on a piece of paper, and don't you lose the money."

"Where'm I going?" asked Sébastien, with evident bad faith.

Victorine, having undone the carefully assembled scaffolding of baskets and debated with herself whether to buy one, had chosen the very smallest.

"Here, I'll take this one."

"Fine," said Angelina curtly.

Sébastien had a stubborn and argumentative side, which never failed to exasperate her. Piling up her baskets again, without daintiness this time, she explained to Sébastien while trying to stay calm:

"Go to Sidonie... She'll find you everything I need."

Mustering all his dignity, Sébastien was crossing the marketplace towards Sidonie's display against the apse of the church.

"Eh!" cried Jean. "Don't go buying nougat with that money! It's thread and buttons Angelina's after."

Sébastien shrugged his shoulders ostentatiously, to make it quite clear that this unnecessary instruction in no way threatened his dignity, and bravely waded into the group of children waiting in ambush behind a buttress of the church. At once, the rhythmical chant resumed:

"Sé-bas-tien, gyp-sy boy! ... Sé-bas-tien, gyp-sy boy...!"

Only this time, old César was there, chatting with two of his peers.

"Mind your ears, you lot!" he cried sharply.

His voice froze the innocent tormentors. Then, with a flutter of capes, the group of children scattered. Victorine said, in a low voice, as if touching on a forbidden subject:

"Now tell me... what does your grandfather think of all this?"

"Sometimes he acts as if he can't hear, but don't you worry! Especially considering it's not the first time it's happened."

Angelina's loud voice must have carried all the way to César.

"Maybe that's why Sébastien doesn't like coming down to the village," said Jean. "Many's the Saturday he prefers staying on his own, up there, at the house, to coming to market."

Victorine nodded:

"Ah well," she said, philosophically, "it teaches him about life, the little lad… Here, lass, the money for my basket…"

She held out the money to Angelina with a slight hesitation:

"Mind you, it's pricey, this little basket!"

Angelina was about to reply sharply, but Victorine had taken Sébastien's side. She contained herself:

"Well," she said, "you're choosing the finest. It took me eight days to make, that one."

"Ah yes," acknowledged Victorine, who knew very well the cost of labour, "but just because we're friends doesn't mean we can't haggle."

Delighted with her purchase, she returned to her market stall.

"Been selling well?" she asked the young girl who helped her in her work.

"Can't complain."

Victorine, reassured, began tidying away her goods, when she noticed Sébastien, right there in front of her, his nose level with a jar of barley sugar, frowning. He seemed to be doing calculations in his head.

"No sweeties, Sébastien! You were told: thread, needles and buttons. Sidonie is over there. Go on, shoo…"

Sébastien, of course, knew it perfectly well. However, it was not as if sweets would melt from being looked at. He hesitated, just for a moment: should he, as his pride demanded, stare down Victorine, or smile at her? His better angel made him choose the second path. After which, he ran away from the tempting jars. Victorine felt a change of heart; she grabbed a packet of sweets.

"Here, lad! Here! They're sour sweets, just the way you like them. Go on, take them!"

Honestly, Sébastien pointed out:

"I can't pay for them."

"Silly goose! I'm giving them to you! Go on, scarper, out of my sight…"

Sébastien went on his way. He was eating his sweets when he arrived in front of the toy-seller's trestle. There were all manner of things, but what he liked was a little watermill with a turning wheel. This was exactly what he wanted for that experiment that he was trying to conduct on the Gordolasque River, uphill from the village, in a bend where the stream was quiet. He looked at his hands: one squeezed the money meant for the buttons, needles and thread, the other held the packet of sweets. He sighed: this shopkeeper was not generous like Victorine. Sébastien knew it; as for betraying Angelina's trust, the thought did not even cross his mind.

A few more steps and he passed the eastern end of the church. At once, the juvenile demons of Saint-Martin encircled him. It was Pierre who opened hostilities.

"The gypsy's got sweets!"

He snatched the packet… and passed it to Antoine. A leg jutted out and tripped Sébastien. The money rolled away, while Antoine, throwing caution to the wind, called out:

"Who wants sour sweets?"

A great roar sounded above the din: it came from Victorine, who, with her arms full of jars, was leaving her market stall and heading back to her shop. She lay everything on the ground.

"Watch them for me…" she said to her assistant.

And Victorine's bulk waded into the scrimmage. By chance, she caught Pierre, even as she yelled at Antoine:

"You give him back my sour sweets, or I'll have a word with your father!"

The disappearance, in a wild eddy, of caps and capes and scarves was almost miraculous. For a second time, Sébastien found himself master of the battlefield. However, he had been helped. It hurt his pride.

"Come on," said big-hearted Victorine, "I'll give you some other sweets."

His money recovered, Sébastien replied with fiery eyes and hard-set lips:

"Don't want any."

And this time, he went running to Sidonie's shop. Victorine was glued to the spot.

"Look at him, the wild thing!" she cried. "Aren't I the soppy one?"

This mocking of her affection made her fickle, and she added:

"Ah, he's typical of his race!"

It was a poisoned dart in Sébastien's heart that filled it with a bit more feral pride. However, when he came back to Angelina's side, he found César, and the pleasure of feeling himself amongst his own calmed him. He wanted only to go back up to the house on the mountain, far from the village. He took Angelina's hand and slipped his small, rough paw into it.

"Can we go now, can we?"

Nimble Angelina bent towards the child, placed a kiss on his amber cheek and whispered into his ear:

"Sébastien, have you seen the doctor?"

"Yes," affirmed Sébastien aloud... "Yesterday, with you!"

"But this morning?"

"Not seen him."

He added, to put things straight:

"The others make fun of me because he looked after my goat..."

This had the effect of exasperating Angelina. She glared aggressively at the market that was ending and, addressing the entire village beyond it, she cried:

"And you wonder why!"

Jean said jokingly:

"Because you sent him to fetch Guillaume instead of the vet – why do you think?"

Angelina, feeling got at, lashed out:

"Oh, you and your stupid laugh! What's funny about it? I know the doctor well, but the vet... not so much. What's more, I don't see why I should hide it."

"So Guillaume looks after goats, now?"

Angelina threw her arms around a monstrous pile of baskets.

"What's so extraordinary about that? So, are you going to help me or are you just going to stand there and laugh?"

It was at this moment that Destiny chose to approach Sébastien in the form of a drum roll. In the silence that followed, he heard Carmagnole, the police ranger, intone:

"Warning to the population: A large dog of exceptional strength, answering to the name 'Belle', is roaming the mountain. It was spotted in Manosque, at Ryons, and yesterday at La Demoiselle. The animal is dangerous. Whoever sees it is authorized to shoot it."

The drum rolled a second time, and Carmagnole, blissfully unaware of his role as an agent of fate, or of the demons he had just let loose in Sébastien's soul, walked farther on to repeat his message.

Later, Jean would remember having instinctively placed his hand on little Sébastien's head, as if to protect him, and how César, with his pipe in his mouth, coolly as was his custom, had watched Carmagnole for a long time, until the village drum had turned the corner of the church. Yes, all of this they would one day recall, but that morning they felt no premonition of dramatic events, close as they were. A voice called them back from their faint disquiet. It belonged to Célestine, a countrywoman who ran the doctor's household with a pride that she made no attempt to disguise. Accustomed to running her domain, and going on the principle that the doctor, together with the mayor, the priest and the police inspector, constituted the area's ruling elite, she made it her job to dictate to the whole village. For this reason, she offered her opinion in a loud voice:

"Well now, that's all we need! What are they waiting for, I ask you, to destroy that animal? For it to devour a child?"

The butcher's assistant, who was carrying a quarter of mutton to the shop on his shoulders, stopped:

"The mountain is big, Madame Célestine. The animal is not necessarily near by."

"Holy Mother of God! Too bad for the neighbours, then – is that what you mean?"

"No, that's not what I mean!"

"Well, it's what you're saying."

The assistant gave a sigh: not to be able to answer the customer back, even when she exasperates you! What a trial, Mother of God! Luckily, Célestine was now having a go at Jean:

"Eh, where's that sister of yours? I need a basket."

Jean pointed to Angelina, visible to all, though partly hidden by the mule, and it was Sébastien who answered back:

"She's still here and you know it!"

The worst thing about Célestine was that you could never guess how she would react: against all expectations, she gave the little boy a radiant smile.

"Eh! Of course I know it, little pigeon!"

Then, with her gendarme's gait, she walked to the mule now loaded with baskets. Everything had to come off, down to the last basket. She spoke at length about the uses intended for this purchase, only in the end to choose one that Angelina had been holding in her hand when Célestine had come over.

Around them, everyone was talking:

"The best thing," said one man, "would be to organize a beat and kill that beast before it does any harm."

He had emphasized the word "beast". He was the first to call her that. His name was Georges and he worked as a carter in Saint-Martin: he hauled wood and took parcels to the station, with his sleigh in winter, with his old cart in the summer, but always with the same horse, unfairly named Carcass, for it had the thick and smooth pelt of a well-fed animal. He, then, was the first to call Belle "the Beast". In addition, he was also the first person Sébastien came to hate. Why? Perhaps because, deep down, he felt a kinship with this Belle who ran free on the mountain, away from people.

Sébastien's imagination flew far from the market, far from his own body. It is cold on the mountain, you feel hungry and alone. Sébastien had known this ever since César first told him about the Baou and the high peaks. That is, he had always spoken about them, since César started when Sébastien was scarcely able to talk. And who knows, maybe he began sooner – Sébastien could not remember. Belle! Carmagnole had said her name… Animals die in the mountains in winter, César finds them buried under the snow, killed by hunger and the cold. And Sébastien discovered suddenly that he did not want Belle to die.

"All the same," says Moulin, the woodcutter, "I'm not going up there again without my gun."

A hand settles on the shoulder of Sébastien, who spins round at the sound of César's voice:

"What's on your mind, Sébastien?"

The child does not answer. He listens to the loud, high voice of Célestine and he can't stand it.

"A vicious beast must be destroyed – that's all there is to it!"

César replies to the doctor's housekeeper:

"Who told you she's vicious?"

And Sébastien smiles, reassured that César is siding with Belle.

"A free animal is not vicious," César adds.

However, it is impossible, in front of everyone, to silence Célestine:

"Sorry, César: you know the mountain better than me – only I do have ears… Carmagnole said it was a dangerous animal. It must be destroyed."

Now Sébastien walks up to Célestine. His ears are red and his eyes shining. He stands before her, his stubborn little forehead raised high and the great mountain behind him.

"I don't want anyone to touch her!"

With that, he runs away as if never to return to the village, as if he too were escaping from a prison.

"Oh, César," said an elder, "you shouldn't let the lad say that."

Jean leapt at this:

"We won't let him get away with it – don't you worry."

César's voice interrupted him:

"Jean… Leave him be. That child is not like the others. He's the son of the mountain."

He in turn brought all his calm authority into play and defended Belle and Sébastien.

Célestine was indignant.

"Not like the others! Well now! A good spanking never hurt anybody, and believe me, César…"

However, César did not believe her. He was busy listening to the schoolmaster, who had come up to him and was saying what César had heard so often since September:

"When are you going to send him to school?"

The old man drew on his pipe:

"Soon, Headmaster… It's hard work, putting a young fox in a cage…"

He had a clever idea on this theme:

"You have to prepare them... Otherwise, some of them waste away or go mad!"

César tended to think that Sébastien needed raising like a fox cub: a peculiar vision that the schoolmaster had no time for.

"He'll come to school in the spring, César – just remember that..."

Sébastien was running along the path. He slowed, stopped entirely, looked around... Nobody! How he hated the village. He left the path and, pushing into a dense cluster of firs, went looking for the mountain stream. You had to meet it quite some way from the village if you wanted to be alone, yet downstream from the Saut-du-Loup when it emerges from the gorge and calms down a little. It was here that Sébastien had constructed, one after the other, two watermills. An early snowmelt had carried off the first. The fate of the second had been no better, only this time it was due to the heavy rains that had beaten down on the mountain. A third still needed building. To study the matter better, he sat on one of the enormous rocks that lined an inlet where the roaring flow of the Gordolasque came to sleep as peacefully as in a pond. He lay on his belly on the rock and leant forward to reach the icy water with his bare hands. It was fun: you got to be a bit like a salmon or a trout.

"Careful, Sébastien: you'll fall in."

Sébastien looked up and, in spite of what troubled him, smiled at Doctor Guillaume, whom he liked.

"I built a mill here," he said, "and it's gone."

The doctor explained in all seriousness:

"You probably didn't weigh it down enough."

"I did."

Guillaume looked at the stubborn face, that immense, golden stare:

"No. Because when I was your age, I made some that stayed in place whole winters without getting carried away, and they were still spinning with the first buds."

Imperturbably, Sébastien gave his opinion:

"Ah! That's hard to believe."

Still as seriously, Guillaume explained:

"It's all about the wheel, and the stability of the uprights, of course."

Sébastien traced a perfect circle on the rock.

"I'd made a wheel like this, and I'd dug in the uprights there, in the water."

"You got it wrong – you should have put them in dry ground."

"You can't," interrupted Sébastien, "it's frozen solid."

"Listen… I dig down, push the uprights in and then add water so that when it freezes, my frame is fixed as if it were in cement. What do you bet? I'll make one that lasts till spring."

Sébastien hesitated: on the one hand, he wanted his mill, on the other, he could not be sure that Guillaume would not bet something too valuable, something that Sébastien would not wish to give him, like the water pistol that Angelina refused to allow him to play with and that he had hidden in the stable, at the far end of the mule's rack, just where a piece of stone was missing... For he knew Guillaume well: he never played with children as the other grown-ups did: it was always in earnest, between equals. Therefore, if there were a bet, if he accepted the wager, there would be no way out or leniency. Weighing for and against, Sébastien knitted his brows. Finally, he gave a loud sniff. He had made up his mind.

"All right," he said.

He was worried, but a watermill that lasts until spring – that was worth a pistol, wasn't it?

Guillaume opened his knife; he put down his doctor's bag that he carried on his shoulder like a rucksack, in order to keep his hands free during the long mountain hikes that his visits obliged him to make. He was returning from one of them just now: old Tonelli was unwell, the winter was hard on him; for three days now, he had been in the grip of a fever and there was no way of persuading him to let himself be taken to hospital. Guillaume knew perfectly well that he would die up there, in his little house on the flank of La Demoiselle. He might make it through this winter, but the next...

"Look," said Sébastien, "here's some wood."

There was no shortage of wood on the banks of the Gordolasque River. Guillaume paused, chose a piece himself and took back Sébastien's:

"This will do for the wheel, but when it comes to the uprights, I'll choose for myself. To get it just right, I'll need some acacia."

"All right."

Sébastien watched admiringly with a connoisseur's eye: a single sweep of the blade, sharp, quick, and the twigs gave way. There was no denying that Guillaume was clever with his hands. However, he was also a systematic thinker:

"Sébastien, you haven't told me what you were betting, in case my mill holds up."

All the subtle cunning that Sébastien possessed went to work, somewhere in his brain. He took on an air of profound detachment:

"I don't really know... a cheese from my goat?"

"No deal," said Guillaume plainly. "It's Angelina who makes the cheeses. I'm not having a bet with Angelina. Choose something of your own."

This was exactly what Sébastien had feared! Guillaume went on whittling admirable little paddles: the mill would surely hold up until spring and then… and then he, Sébastien, would lose the bet and Guillaume would never forget it!

"Tell you what," said Guillaume, so perfectly innocent that he would have duped one of God's angels, "you go to school next Easter if the mill is still standing."

With the nimble movement of a bird taking flight, Sébastien was up:

"Ah, no, not that!"

Guillaume folded up his knife abruptly.

"It's up to you… The mill can be for another time."

The angelic gaze of those big golden eyes lifted slowly from the knife to the doctor's face.

"That lot," said Sébastien, "call me 'the gypsy'… They're all at school. I don't want to see them."

Looking as if he understood, Guillaume went on:

"They make fun of you because you refuse to play with them – you brush them off. You only care for the mountain, so they say you're proud. Stop hiding away in your own corner and you'll see."

Gravely, Sébastien sifted for the truth in this information. It satisfied his dignity.

"It's sort of true," he admitted. "I don't like going down to the village. There are too many people."

Forgetting his childish cunning, he burst out straight from his heart:

"You know, apart from you, and then César and Angelina and Jean, I don't like anyone."

For an instant, Guillaume was on the verge of giving up the fight and building the mill for nothing.

"What a strange little fellow you are!"

Face to face, man and child had forgotten the game they had meant to play. However, it was the man who first mastered his emotions: what would become of Sébastien if no one helped him become a little more like other people? In all the wide world, there is no room for wild and rebellious little boys.

"Well then, Sébastien, are you betting or not?"

The little one looked up in anguish:

"Do we really have to bet?"

A twinge in the doctor's heart overturned his certainty. He lowered his gaze, reopened his knife and with its point sent a splinter of wood furiously flying.

"Yes," he said.

It was a heavy price for Sébastien! Why was Guillaume obliging him to bet? Would he, too, come to be like the others, making speeches and talking reproachfully? Sébastien would not have been able to find the words to express it, but he sensed that there was a little bit of cowardice in all of this, and that cowardice was not his way. So, with the pride that came naturally to him, he muttered:

"Right. Agreed."

Guillaume made sure of his victory, a victory that looked far into Sébastien's future…

"You'll go to school if my mill is running in the spring?"

Sébastien's candid little paw stretched out:

"Put it there!"

And Guillaume felt ashamed. A little sad as well: he knew that he had gained authority in the child's mind, but that he had just lost a portion of his heart. This made him lose himself in his work. He must have had a lot of experience with watermills on the Gordolasque, and rare skill: the meticulous work advanced quickly, and Sébastien, filled with wonder, came to forget the hardness of men and the price that this work of art would demand of him.

Moreover, the mill wheel turned! It would turn for a long time yet… The doctor went down towards the village, and the child went back up the path to the house. All of a sudden, he turned a luminous smile on the snow-covered mountain, at the blue of the sky… as if he were sending a greeting to the great wandering dog that everyone called fierce because it walked, free, somewhere in all that emptiness. Sébastien shouted out her name, just to try it, to see what effect it would have. The village bell answered him, ringing the hour. It seemed very near, and yet so far away, lost in the vastness of the mountain. Sébastien called out again:

"Belle…"

He did not notice that he was going straight up towards "his" mountain, following the goat track, leaving behind the house, César and the family. When he realized, he was already high up, and besides, it was past dinner time! Now Sébastien slowed his pace, rejoicing with an untroubled mind in the rough rocks and the pine needles that formed, where the snow failed to cover them, a soft and fragrant layer under his boots. He knew his mountain, all right! In truth, it was all that he knew. From the Baou to the Demoiselle, it had always been there. He loved it. He knew its faces, all the expressions it can wear according to the season and the time of day. This makes for an infinity of different mountains – a hundred, a thousand, all with summits from which the vast sweep gradually descends and precipices plunge into the gorges. The rocky moraine stricken by summer sun is not the one that winter burdens with snow, nor that of spring, when flowers seem to hatch from the stones, when all the scents mingle amid the buzzing of bees and the mistle thrush bursts into song.

Moreover, the nights, the soft nights of moonlight that make the slopes whiter and deepen the mystery of the chasm where the Gordolasque roars, are nothing like the terrible nights, when the howling wind knocks at the doors and windows, and Sébastien, in bed, feels the old house trembling. So much so that one wonders, at dawn, how the world can still be the same, how it has not been transformed, overturned to such an extent that it ought to be impossible to recognize it.

Sébastien loved all of these faces. It was only in them and through them that he was truly happy. César would not allow him to go beyond the fork that the road makes in summer, where it snakes around the Baou and ascends towards the customs post, leaving on the left the path of the Grand Défilé, which the elders call the "corridor of doom", because, each year during the thaw, avalanches rumble there, shattering everything in their path. Sébastien had never disobeyed. Besides, by the time he had got up as far as the fork, he was far too tired to go any farther, and César had taught him to conserve his energy, and how to come back down at the same pace as he had gone up.

Yes, Sébastien knew all these things. He also knew how to recognize the animals of the solitudes that those who live down below are unable to see. What did he care for the alphabet that Angelina was determined to teach him, since he could tell the story of a footprint covered in snow? What were numbers to him, since he knew the birds that live in pairs from those that flock together? The truth was that Sébastien was far more knowledgeable than those who went to school. He gave a heavy sigh: Easter would come quickly, and he would go to school and all the time he spent there would be so much time lost to the patient discoveries that César had always taught him to make on his mountain... but a promise is a promise!

Up until the crossing through the spruce wood, Sébastien had followed Doctor Guillaume's footprints. Now that they veered off towards Tonelli's house, he left them behind. However, before undertaking the climb in the pristine snow that no one had yet walked in today, he turned to face the valley. The village looked flattened, a carpet of rooftops from which rose thin columns of smoke. There was no wind: the smoke flew straight up. It was funny to imagine everyone in their houses, busily putting wood in the fireplace or sitting at their tables. Sébastien felt he was so much taller than them!

He started walking again and reached the heap of bare rocks that people call the "Giant's Game". The rocks are so big that, when walking alongside one of them, you can see nothing more than a high wall topped with a layer of snow that drips away slowly to form a jagged edge of ice. A lump of snow fell behind him and, almost at the same moment, a pebble ricocheted off the rock face. Sébastien turned around. He was alone.

He walked on, moving from rock to rock as if through a labyrinth. Another stone fell. It sank into the snow with a ponderous softness. Sébastien looked up, making himself very still. He knew how to listen to and interpret the smallest sounds, but heard only the light breeze in the sleeping silence of the snow. Therefore, he went on, beyond the heap of rocks, and reached the great rock face that was too steep for snow to cling to. Suddenly, he threw himself against the cliff, narrowly avoiding a mass of snow that crashed almost soundlessly in front of him. This time he was sure of it: someone was on his trail, someone who could hide at will behind the rocks or reach the overhang of the rock face, and he was afraid. He was just under the ledge, and this was where the snow had fallen. He eased himself away from the rock, gingerly. He looked up…

…and saw her. Right above him. She was watching him, and her large silhouette stood out against the frozen blue of the sky.

Sébastien wiped his eyes with the back of his hand. There she was, standing tall, motionless save for the plume of her tail as it beat the air. Vapour came out of the half-open chops with their long black outline; two more black lines made her eyes stand out in the golden whiteness of her fur. She saw him. She bent her head towards him. Was she going to jump? He no longer felt any fear, and if he too stood still it was because an unknown force compelled him to hold his ground before the animal now watching him. He called to her very softly:

"Belle..."

She did not move, but her tail continued to wag as she watched him. So he steeled himself and took a few steps forward. The only audible thing in the great silence was the creaking of the snow under his feet.

"Come! Come with me!"

She appeared to be listening. Was it him, or some other noise from below that she alone could detect? Or maybe the distant rumble of the mountain stream? All of a sudden, she disappeared. She melted, white, into the whiteness of the snow. She was climbing higher, towards the Baou, and the mountain wind carried off what Sébastien was calling out to Belle... To Belle as she fled from Sébastien's enchanted gaze.

Back home, he could think of nothing to say. The mill on the torrent, Guillaume, school, all of it was forgotten. Sébastien dropped his gaze, his throat constricting under Angelina's reproaches. He kept quiet.

"We looked everywhere for you. You've never been out that long! And with that animal on the loose on the mountain… Grandfather is still out looking for you, and just you wait for the smack Jean is going to give you when he gets back from work! Aren't you ashamed of yourself for giving us such a fright?"

César only came back in the evening, at the same time as Jean. Angelina had just put Sébastien to bed. With eyes shut, he pretended to be asleep when César bent over him. A flutter of his eyelids gave him away… whereupon César sat on the edge of the bed and placed a hand on his brown hair.

"Sébastien…"

He opened his eyes. César looked into them as if they were full of visible pictures… until his smile stole over the little one's face:

"You know…"

César's light blue gaze became keener than ever: "I know."

He spoke low and calmly, and Sébastien closed his eyes again. So César continued:

"Sébastien… you don't want them to kill that animal?"

What Sébastien saw in his mind's eye was too beautiful… He did not open his eyes and, with the strength of his newfound love, replied:

"No."

"Why?"

"I don't know."

"And yet you don't know this dog."

Under their thick white lashes, the eyes of the old man were smiling. Sébastien turned his face to the wall.

"I don't want them to, that's all."

The little spark of jollity in César's blue gaze went out slowly. He was solemn when he said:

"Sleep, lad… If you don't want anyone to harm that animal, no one will harm her."

This time, Sébastien turned his head and looked at the old man: from here on, everything would be easy!

It was a clear and quiet night that neither gusts of wind nor the groans of the old house could disturb. Everything slept now. Sébastien got out of bed. The frost traced arabesques on the window panes; they could have been spruce branches, or bracken, or splashes of starlight. A hot little hand melted the lot, and Sébastien waited.

The clock struck midnight. Sébastien continued to wait, pinched by the cold but certain that she would come. She had to.

And she did come. It began with a low and gentle howl that filled the night with its sadness. At last, he saw her appear on the ridge that dominated the house to the north. She passed by slowly, whiter still in the moonlight than she had been during the day. So beautiful that, long after she had gone, Sébastien continued to smile into the night.

3

In Provence, people talk, but cruelty is far from their hearts.

Down in the village, folk might not have attached such importance to the "Beast's" presence on the mountain, and Belle would have regained the peace that she had earned on reaching the heights, if Michel Boudu had not had his adventure, and if Belle had not stolen that leg of lamb.

Michel, who was the son of Saint-Martin's wheelwright, was more than a little proud of his skiing skills. These skills were relative, given that he was ten years old, but they had earned him a new pair of skis. So one fine morning he went to try them out on the slopes above the course of the Gordolasque –

those very slopes where, the day before, Sébastien had encountered Belle.

The church had just sounded the last stroke of noon, and in the wheelwright's household everyone was raging already against Michel's lateness, but since no one was thinking any more about Belle, the only expressions of worry concerned the son's deplorable tendency to make his father wait for his dinner. In the end, the family gathered around the table, where the mother, Rose Boudu, set down the dish of expertly simmered *pieds et paquets*.

It was at this moment that the Boudus' eldest opened the front door like a whirlwind. He scarcely had time to lean the costly pair of new skis against the outside wall before his entrance raised a storm:

"I've seen the—"

"Shut the door," interrupted Boudu.

Michel obeyed, regretting that the impact of his news had been thus diminished. More modestly, he resumed:

"I've seen the—"

"Where've you been?" asked his mother. "And why are you so late?"

Disconcerted, Michel could only answer:

"I was at the municipal ski jump…"

This was thin gruel for a boy who wanted to fill every ear in the village with his news, but how could he avoid answering so specific a question?

"Well then. Is it too much for you to come home on time?" said the father, as he filled his son's plate with *pieds et paquets*.

"And to think I punished you for it yesterday," said the mother, getting up to reach the bottle of wine on the sideboard.

Everyone went quiet, the better to savour Rose Boudu's wonderful cooking. Then, in the respectful silence:

"What did you see?" asked his little sister, Janine.

Bashful now, Michel replied dully:

"I saw the Beast."

Even so, he hoped this would have the impact of a bomb.

"Oh, that's a good one!" exclaimed Rose Boudu. "Only yesterday you were late, you dreamt up I don't know what excuse, and today you've seen the Beast?"

"Yesterday," Michel explained, "I was looking for its tracks. Today I found them."

This time the effect exceeded his best hopes:

"Holy Mother!" cried Rose Boudu. "Did you hear that? Hippolyte, did you hear? Shall I fetch your gun?"

Boudu senior wiped his chin and the moustache that gave him a piratical air – a look that belied the gentleness of his eyes.

"Just a minute, Rose! Let me talk to the lad!"

Having reasserted his marital and paternal authority, Pa Boudu began questioning:

"So, you say you've seen the Beast?"

Michel, whose mouth was full, nodded, and this was enough to unbridle his mother's imagination:

"Hippolyte! Are you listening to him, man? What have we got a municipal council for?"

Pa Boudu being a municipal councillor, this was a head-on attack. He replied as his sense of honour demanded:

"The council's got other things to worry about."

"Other things? Holy Mary! Mother of God! Other things than the lives of your children? Hippolyte, I tell you – I can't make you out."

However, Janine was following her own train of thought:

"The Beast, is it big?"

"I saw it from far away," Michel confessed, his mouth full again.

He swallowed his last mouthful and explained:

"She was on the lookout, but even so, she must have smelt me! She turned around, looking mean, and then she went off towards the Baou."

Rose Boudu, her arms outstretched and her face a picture of tragedy, cried out in horror:

"God! She would have eaten him! Let me fetch your gun!"

"Oh!" said Janine, who was tender-hearted.

"What do you mean, 'oh'?" said her father indignantly. "When this beast comes down to the village, on account of being starved, will you still say 'oh' then?"

All were silent with their thoughts. The only sound was of the Boudus' teeth crunching apples. Finally, Rose stood up, took the coffee pot from the edge of the stove and reached for a basket of walnuts.

"Hippolyte! Why don't you go and warn the council?"

"I have work to do! Send Michel… When it comes to warnings, there's no one can touch him!"

Rose flung her arms about her son.

"You'd let him go out? You'd send your own son to his death? Hippolyte, you have no heart!"

"Come now, this beast's not in the streets yet!"

Thus the people of Saint-Martin were reminded of the problem, and of the imminence of danger: the Beast was prowling on the mountain – Michel Boudu had seen it! This was said, repeated and exaggerated every time. Before the day was over, people were expecting the worst. Agitation spread from neighbour to neighbour; it was as if the fine pink stones of the houses were saying, "Michel Boudu has seen the Beast! Michel Boudu has seen the Beast!" And when Victorine was sure of it, having interrogated Michel, the cry she let out might have been audible as far as César's house.

"The Beast, Madame Daniéli! It's here! The one that devoured its keeper, the ferocious beast!"

Madame Daniéli was hard of hearing. Nevertheless, she managed eventually to make out a sound. Not knowing what it consisted of exactly, she contented herself with an "Oh!" of apparent understanding, whereupon she hurried to Sidonie to announce that Victorine was as panicked as a bird in a thunderstorm.

At Sidonie's shop, everyone was already discussing the news, and this was where Célestine came to hear of it. Leaving the gossips, she raced back to the doctor's house and went straight into his consulting room. He had just come back and was working at his desk.

"What's the matter, Célestine?"

"Michel Boudu has seen the Beast…"

"I know, I've already heard."

He returned to his writing. It was a somewhat cavalier way in which to receive the news. Appalled, Célestine quickly gauged how she might make it more striking and more personal:

"I suppose they also told you that it was up by old César's house that Michel saw the Beast…"

It was untrue, but Dr Guillaume had to be roused one way or another! Guillaume looked up:

"No," he said, suddenly interested. "No, I didn't know that."

Célestine was delighted.

"That's what I came to tell you."

Relishing her revenge, she said as an aside:

"For supper, you'll have the cold lamb and the olive tart. I've nothing more to say."

"That's fine, Célestine, you know very well I appreciate your cooking."

"My cooking, perhaps, but my conversation… Mind you, I know when to keep quiet."

"On the contrary, Célestine, I'd like to hear what you know about this story."

Célestine brushed imaginary dust from the bookcase. She was as pleased with the turn of the conversation as an angler is to feel a gudgeon wriggling at the end of his line. She could have quivered with pleasure!

"Which 'story' is monsieur referring to?"

She had made use of the third person! This happened only on serious occasions. Guillaume had retained enough of his childhood self to make him sometimes naive, but not to the point of failing to notice that Célestine was playing the innocent.

"The matter of the Beast," he said briefly. "What's your view?"

It was a way of granting victory to his house-keeper. Forgetting her resentment, she placed her-self in the doorway:

"What do I think? Quite simply, that a vicious beast must be destroyed."

"It may not be a vicious beast, just a hungry one."

"And the keeper it nearly killed, over there… where it came from?"

"Killed? No, Célestine. It knocked him over."

"I didn't say that it killed him, Monsieur, I said 'nearly' killed. Yes, Monsieur, nearly! I read it in the newspaper. And it will kill others. And you, the local doctor, do nothing!"

She waited a moment before firing her final dart:

"You'll think the same as me when it's eaten Sébastien, what with him wandering about all the time, the innocent! Come now: you know very well that the mountain may have witnessed the little one's birth, but she is not going to mother him…"

The doctor was suddenly harsh:

"Sébastien is not on his own, Célestine."

Indignation, bitterness, jealousy made the house-keeper lose all sense of proportion, and she fired her ammunition in all directions:

"I know as well as you do that Angelina is a fine girl… and pretty – you're a better judge of that than me – but she is young! And then, that beast, it's a danger to everyone, to her as for others!"

This persuaded Guillaume to get up, to open the door and put on his fur-lined cloak. Célestine began to whine:

"And when will you be having my supper? Because if you're setting out now... when will you be back?"

However, Guillaume was no longer listening to her:

"I'm going up to the house, Célestine. I have to speak to César."

The door, shut by Célestine, made a distinctly disapproving noise.

"César is an old fool," she declared to the entire house and added for her own comfort:

"But his gun shoots straight."

César's gunshot, let off near the Baou refuge, echoed for a long time. Sébastien, with his nose in the air, listened to the strange echo that so breaks up the sound that it seems to come back at you from several places at once. However, what interested him most of all was the straight fall of the bird.

"Got it... It's fallen behind the rock!"

He ran, so light a figure that he coasted over the soft snow, towards the bird of prey that César had just shot. The old man followed him more slowly.

"It's a white eagle," cried Sébastien. "You've killed a white eagle... You shouldn't have!"

César picked up the corpse, considered the scale of it.

"No, look at these brown markings on the end of the wings. It's a peregrine falcon. A very handsome bird. As a juvenile it's almost brown, but the older it gets, the whiter it becomes."

The old man held in his hand the little head with its beak that was curved and barbed like a weapon.

"It's the noblest of the great birds of prey; it flies straight at its quarry, never bluffing, from way up high where it likes to live and build its nest... Yes, it's the only noble bird of prey. You're right: I shouldn't have fired... And yet, if they're noble, they're dangerous if they become too numerous. They don't hesitate to attack a lamb – and lambs, you know, also have the right to live."

Sébastien listened, his intelligent gaze lifted towards the old man:

"How do you know all this?"

César smiled. This understanding between himself and Sébastien was his great joy. The child he had taken in was closer to him, at certain moments, than his own flesh and blood. Under the white thicket of his eyebrows, his clear eyes swept lovingly across the vast expanse of snow, the high ridge of the Baou. They came back to settle on the serious little face:

"I was a game warden for such a long time in the mountains that—"

"Here?" interrupted Sébastien.

"No. A long way from here…"

César gestured with his chin towards the east…

"There's a lot more forest there than we have."

"And mountains?" Sébastien interrupted again.

"Some very high mountains. There are even animals that once lived in our parts but now only survive there."

"Ah!" said Sébastien.

Mountains higher and wilder than the Baou! Try as he might, he could not imagine what they looked like.

"And did you come back to the house a long time ago?"

73

"I came back when Angelina was a little girl and Jean was practically a baby... when I lost my daughter and my son-in-law..."

Once more, his eyes roamed across the great snow-covered moraine.

"My daughter was the mother of Angelina and Jean."

"Ah!" said Sébastien again.

He was too young to understand: he saw only the sadness in César's blue eyes. He lowered his own towards the white remains of the bird: César was binding its talons with a cord. The silence grew heavy, but Sébastien knew that some silences are not to be broken: they are as fragile as glass, and behind them there is great sorrow that can only be contained with difficulty.

They took the path back, and César's voice had regained its usual composure as he slipped the little cord that bound the big bird across his shoulder:

"I'll fix it up and we'll keep it in the big room at the house. It's a fine specimen. Aren't you tired? We've walked a long way today."

Their footsteps barely disturbed the silence of the snow, and it was possible to hear César's rifle knocking regularly against his leg.

"I've never come this far," said the child when they arrived at the centre of the cirque surrounded by peaks.

The sound of the waterfall stopped Sébastien in his tracks.

"For you, this is the edge of the world."

César looked at the mountain. He went up to Sébastien and gently placed a hand on his head:

"Here we are, you see, on the other side of the Baou... Now let's hurry, night is falling and Angelina will start to worry. It's time to go home."

"Look: there's a refuge. Aren't we going that way?"

César seemed to hesitate, and then replied calmly:

"If you like."

The going became difficult, snow clinging loosely to the rocky scree. Above them was a great sweep of enormous stones.

"You see all those rocks," said César, "with every avalanche a few more come down. This is where the Grand Défilé ends up... and that way, if we went on, we'd get to the customs post."

"And the refuge," Sébastien persisted, "what's it for?"

César, his eyes fixed on the large black cross that stood near the refuge, replied:

"It's for nobody... not for a long time."

He added, as if he meant to wipe away with his words memories that Sébastien did not yet need to share:

"On the other side, that's Italy. There, at the end of the Petit Défilé, lies the border... And here's the Demoiselle..."

He lowered his arm, having just pointed in each direction.

"Come on."

"What's the border?" asked Sébastien. "Is it a line?"

"In a way."

"How do you get there?"

"Where the track passes through the Petit Défilé, it goes up between the Demoiselle and the Baou. But only in summer – in winter, as you well know, it's all under snow."

"And there's no other way?"

"If you're a bird, you can fly, and if you want to die, you take the Grand Défilé."

"Ah!" said Sébastien after a moment. "Is it so dangerous?"

"Yes, my boy – it's a corridor of avalanches... 'The corridor of doom'. I've told you about it, remember."

"That's true, I know it from down below, but up here I don't recognize anything."

They had reached the refuge and were skirting around it. Sébastien pulled César by the hand.

"Let's go in and see..."

César looked at the child. He stood still and, taking out his supply of tobacco and his pipe, peacefully stuffed it.

"No," he said finally, "nobody goes into this refuge any more."

Sébastien was disappointed:

"Why?"

César lit his pipe before answering:

"Out of respect... A woman died there, nearly seven years ago."

Sébastien, his brows knitted in thought, remarked:

"I'm nearly seven, you know."

César hesitated, then went on:

"This is where you were born, Sébastien. Your mother died bringing you into the world."

Sébastien's nose creased at the same time as his forehead: this was how he looked when he was thinking, but this time, too many incomprehensible notions were bound up in César's words. Sébastien's reasoning led him to one question only:

"Is that why Angelina looks after me?"

"Yes, lad, that's why. We'll go and find her now. Here, take the falcon – we killed it together, it's only fair that you bring it back to the house."

From then on, and for the whole of their journey home, Sébastien had no more questions. The conviction that he was a hunter was enough to occupy his thoughts. From the summit of the first crest, they could see the house. A figure that they both recognized was climbing up the steep path.

"Guillaume… It's Guillaume!" cried Sébastien.

Then a sudden doubt made him ask:

"Once, when he was my age, you killed an eagle – that's what he told me."

"Yes," admitted César.

And, with laughter in his voice, he added:

"But a falcon is almost rarer!"

This chased all worry from Sébastien's mind. They went down to the coomb, then walked back up towards the house.

"Do you think Angelina's going to marry Guillaume?"

César gave no sign of surprise, but there was worry in his look:

"That's what I'd have wished," he said finally. "I would have wished for it in the past, but you have to understand, he's become the doctor and…"

Sébastien was taken aback:

"What does that matter? Ah, I see! She'd live in the village, we'd see less of her and you'd be sad!"

"Yes," César concluded, "yes, you're right. That must be the reason."

It was not that easy to have done with Sébastien:

"So is it true? Is that why you don't want it to happen?"

César always spoke frankly to Sébastien, but this time it was difficult: how to explain the spitefulness of a village to a child, the envy of some, the gossip of others, and then the barriers that separate a local doctor from the granddaughter of a gamekeeper?

Sébastien ended César's ruminations in his usual abrupt manner:

"He's got to get married to Angelina, because otherwise he'll get married to Christine, the mayor's daughter, and I like Angelina better. Because firstly she's much prettier and then... she's Angelina."

He added confidentially:

"And you know, she really likes the doctor, does Angelina."

How to reply without giving rise to a mountain of questions? César preferred to keep quiet.

Angelina was doing the laundry when she heard someone whistle a very familiar tune. Hastily she untied her apron and ran to the mirror hanging on the chimney corner: it reflected a face whose fear of not being sufficiently beautiful could not detract from its beauty. The purity of its classical features and its dusky complexion would have made it severe, were it not lit up by the warm transparency of the eyes: a golden gaze, very light under dark lashes and eyebrows. It was framed by the delicate waving locks of her brown hair. In short, Angelina was very pretty, with that beauty, both lively and composed, which the girls of Provence often develop in infancy. She smiled at the mirror and turned to face the door.

Guillaume was on the threshold.

Since he had returned to the region, having finished his studies, she called him "Doctor" and addressed him formally. He, being perhaps more simple-hearted, called her by her name, "Angelina", and, as in former times, when he was a very young man and she a little girl, and he returned to the village in the school holidays, he addressed her informally.

He looked at her now, happily but shyly. He was in love – that was obvious – but – and Angelina's heart quailed every time this shadow passed across her happiness – César seemed set against it. Did he fear a marriage that, on the surface, was not to the doctor's advantage? Out of pride? Angelina's smile lit up her features. So what if people prattled in the village? She didn't care what spiteful gossips might say out of jealousy at her youthful triumph! With the ardour of a young Victory, she went towards him where he stood on the threshold, blocking it with his height, the vast snowy landscape behind him. She loved him, he loved her, and she was waiting only for him to say it instead of showing it. What did the rest matter?

"Do come in, Doctor…"

She turned back to the fireplace and added a log. Rising sparks bathed her in light.

"Come and warm yourself. It must be cold outside today…"

He went towards the fire; it illuminated the tender frankness of his face and the short cut of his brown hair, which accentuated the Roman aspect of his profile. She made him sit down in César's armchair and went to drape his fur-lined coat and scarf on the sideboard. He for his part watched her kneel beside the hearth and reach for the bellows hanging beside the armchair. The fire was not in need of reviving, but the task allowed her to glance at the serious and handsome face that she loved. They were at that happy stage of love where everything is spoken by a look and nothing has yet been said.

"Is it the goat you've come to see? She's well… so is the mule."

She pretended to be in earnest and her eyes shone with pleasure, making her more attractive still.

Laughter suited Guillaume: it gave away his true age that his work often obscured.

"I know – Sébastien told me… I haven't come to see the goat or the mule…"

"Ah" was all that Angelina said, and something inexpressible constricted her throat.

"…only your grandfather," Guillaume concluded.

"Oh, I see," said Angelina quietly.

She was disappointed and, in a sudden fit of temper, spoke harshly:

"Then you'll have to come back later: he isn't in."

The doctor leant towards the fire.

"Tell me, Angelina... one day, will you let me enter this house for a reason other than the goat, or the mule, or one of Sébastien's colds?"

His tone was curt, for Angelina's last words had left a bitterness in him. For her part, the wave of happiness that had swept over her at his entrance ebbed away. She felt paralysed by a perverse timidity that left her feeling leaden and joyless. Unjustly she made Guillaume bear responsibility for their quarrel:

"How grumpy you are!"

Now that same timidity burst, like a soap bubble, and, herself again, Angelina continued:

"I... I meant to say that my grandfather is very well and that he's gone out on the mountain with Sébastien, without even taking time to finish his lunch... You know what the two of them are like: vagabonds. They can't stay cooped up!"

This revived Guillaume's anxiety and reminded him of his reason for visiting:

"You're sure they've gone together?"

"I'm certain. Sébastien wanted to go to the Baou, and Grandfather has taken him there... What's on your mind?"

Candidly, he replied:

"From what you tell me... If they're together, there's nothing to worry about."

He got up, went to take his coat and scarf from the sideboard.

"Well now, I must be getting back... Goodbye, Angelina."

He hesitated with his hand on the door handle:

"Tell César I'll drop in again this evening, after supper."

Kneeling beside the fireplace, Angelina was motionless.

"Why not wait for him?" she muttered without meeting his eye. "It'll be dark soon: he won't be long."

A flush of joy reddened the young man's face:

"What if someone needs me... a patient?"

She leapt to her feet and watched him frankly. She had her answer ready:

"Madame Célestine will send someone for you – she knows perfectly well that you're here."

"Yes, she knows."

Diffidently, Guillaume added:

"But you – are you sure I am not disturbing you?"

Angelina felt a joyful sort of thrill deep within herself.

"I have to rinse my washing and peg it out in the shed. You can keep me company while I work."

"If you like... I could help you!"

There was so much joy at the heart of these simple words!

"Come on," she said.

And life leapt within her.

César and Sébastien were getting to the summit of the final ridge – the one that projects directly over the house from the north. Night falls fast in December, when afternoons are merely prolonged dusks. In front of them, the house was melting already into the shadows, but the sun's last rays lit up the window of the west gable that was rounded in the form of a dovecote. Above the chimney, scrolls of smoke arose, scarcely troubled by the evening breeze and pale in the dark blue of encroaching night. It was the calm of dusk; a sense of solemnity weighed on the mountain.

Then came the long howl.

How tragically it expressed the terror, the heavy sorrow of life before the day's ending, and it was also the clamour that heralds the hunt! Man and boy stopped in their tracks. Sébastien was transfixed, as on hearing that cry must be the fox at the mouth of its den, the hare in its burrow and, perhaps, on the summit of the Baou, that noble and solitary bird, the falcon.

A sharp sound that he knew well made Sébastien turn his head: César was cocking his rifle. Therefore, the child cupped his hands around his mouth and let fly the long, wavering call of the mountaineer.

Far away, lost in the veils of night and solitude, did Belle hear him, did she want to reply? Again, the harrowing howl sounded... And Sébastien smiled happily. He began again, more quietly, and this time it was an insistent call.

Staring at the child, tensed, as if he had flown out of himself and followed Sébastien's cry, César disarmed his rifle. He slung it over his shoulder from its leather strap, and silence spread again across the mountain. The old man led Sébastien away.

"You wanted to see her again. Is that why you asked me to bring you to the Baou?"

Sébastien bowed his head. Then, in the silence that only the creaking of snow under their feet disturbed:

"Don't be afraid, Sébastien."

With his face turned towards the village, César added:

"Nobody's going to hurt her. I won't allow it."

"She's very beautiful... very white," said the child, in a single breath.

In the house, at the top of the stairs, shone the lamp that Angelina had lit for them to see in case the fog settled. When she heard their footsteps, she opened the door and scolded them gently from the threshold.

"The doctor's been waiting for you for hours! Jean's home already."

"Good evening, César," said Guillaume. "I came up to talk to you."

César handed his gun to Angelina:

"Clean it well, love – it's been fired."

Then he reached out to shake the doctor's hand. Jean was roasting chestnuts in the ashes. He made fun of Sébastien as he proudly showed off the bird:

"That's your game, is it?"

Sébastien stretched out the long pale wings.

"It's a peregrine falcon," he said solemnly.

Angelina took off his jacket and hat. Jean handed Sébastien a burning-hot chestnut and peeled another with his teeth.

"Did you see the Demoiselle in her wedding veil? What about the Lady of the Snows, up on the Baou? Did you see her?"

He spoke clumsily because of the chestnut burning his mouth, then joyfully seized Sébastien and, with the clumsy strength of his seventeen years, held him up in the air at arms length. Sébastien managed to sneak a punch that left Jean flabbergasted.

"Ah! The little savage!" he cried, while Angelina applauded:

"Serves you right!"

César was warming his hands in front of the fire.

"Leave him be," he said to Jean. "He's got ideas in his head today… Fetch me a lantern so I can hang up the falcon in the shed."

Lighting the lantern that Jean held out to him, César said to Guillaume:

"Do you remember the day when I took you to the Baou for the first time? How old were you? Six… seven?"

"I must have been somewhere around seven."

Guillaume added, smiling at his memories and at Sébastien:

"I remember it as if it were yesterday."

César, holding the lit lantern in one hand, picked up the falcon in the other and went towards the door.

"I need a word with you, César," said Guillaume. "I'll come with you."

On the way, he took his fur-lined jacket and scarf. Angelina called after them from the doorway:

"I forgot to give the mule her hay!"

César's voice answered:

"We'll see to it, love."

She watched the light as it went, swaying, towards the barn.

"Shut the door," cried Jean. "It's freezing!"

She obeyed automatically, returning to her cooking as it simmered on a corner of the stove. Sébastien was asleep, sitting in his place at the table, his head resting on his outstretched arms.

"You shouldn't let Grandpa take him so far out on the mountain," said Jean.

Angelina shrugged. She thought the same as her brother, but as she had already said to the doctor, "Those two – like vagabonds!... Jean was never like that."

César set down the lantern and the bird of prey on an empty barrel, then, taking the pitchfork, went to the pile of hay.

"What was she dreaming about, today, to forget her mule?" he grumbled.

Guillaume replied perhaps a little too quickly:

"It was wash day. Angelina had a lot on her plate."

"Ah, yes! The washing!"

A gleam of amusement flashed across César's face: he did not much believe in the washing! He thought it had more to do with Guillaume... He had pushed open the door to the stable that led to the shed, and they were struck as much by the potent smell as by the warmth of the animals. Guillaume went up to Paquita, the mule. As he spoke, he caressed the pretty head with its large, black-lined eyes:

"I wanted to talk to you about the animal that's on the loose on the mountain... the big dog. They say a boy saw it today. It's in the area."

César piled the hay into the racks.

"I know," he said. "We heard her on the way back: she was howling, and it wasn't a happy cry."

"Did you see her?"

"Only heard her. But Sébastien met her one day when he was out alone. She did him no harm... but there it is, he can think of nothing else. You know what children are like, the ideas they get... he's hooked. He loves that animal. Do you understand, Guillaume?"

"And what if she really is dangerous, César? The little tearaway is so often on his own..."

His hand went on mechanically stroking the mule, whose coat gleamed in the glow of the lantern.

"They say it's a Pyrenean dog."

"Aye," said César, "a fine mountain animal, rescue breed."

"So you've seen her too?"

César's eyes blinked under his eyebrows:

"Don't you worry! Old César is watching... What do you think of my peregrine falcon?"

"A fine specimen," conceded the doctor who, returning to his thoughts, added:

"It's Célestine who made me come and find you..."

César stirred the hay of the litter with his pitchfork:

"Your Célestine is nothing but a cackling old magpie!"

This made the doctor laugh.

"She's not so bad!"

He grew serious again:

"Even so, with her, you know what's going on in these parts. And in the village, everyone's talking about the Beast on the loose. If ever she came down to the valley, she'd be shot, or worse – injured."

César had come back into the shed. He stretched out the great wings of the bird and pinned them apart with two nails.

"I'll fix him up and we'll put him in the front room... Right," he said when he had finished. "Now listen to me, Guillaume: tell them, down in the village, that so long as that animal does no more harm than she's done up till now, César is on her side, whatever anyone says! You tell them."

"And yet, César, she did injure a man. I'm not in favour of her being hunted down either... But what if she starts up again?"

César, his face giving nothing away, shrugged his shoulders:

"Sébastien has no mother or father... Children in the village call him 'the gypsy'. He is a little child, and he wants that animal. There. I've said what I have to say. Take the lantern, Doctor, and come."

He said nothing more. He could tell from Guillaume's silence that his words had sunk in, that he had faith in him, and that Belle – the Belle that Sébastien longed for – now had one further ally.

Nevertheless, before giving in, Guillaume insisted.

"César, will you give me your word that Sébastien is in no danger?"

The old man unhooked some salt meat that was hanging from a beam to dry out and showed it to the doctor.

"Old César knows what he's doing. Look at this piece of meat, son: this is better than a gun against a famished animal. Tell that to the village too... and keep the lantern to get you down. You can bring it back to me... next wash day!"

When Guillaume glanced towards the house, he added:

"I'll tell them goodnight for you."

"César..."

The old man cut in:

"You understand, Guillaume – you are 'the doctor'... In a village like ours, that counts. In the old days, when I took you on hikes around the Baou, as I took Sébastien today, things were different: you were a lad like the others."

His voice, having softened, became firm again, almost hard:

"Now, everything's changed. You're someone important: the doctor! Doesn't that sound impressive: the doctor! And the mayor wants to marry off his daughter. He owns some good land, does the mayor! The girl's no worse-looking than any other;

he sent her off to get an education, I don't know where... You understand what I'm saying? So little Angelina doesn't amount to much against all of that. And it's wrong to let a young women dream!"

Ardently, in an almost deep voice, Guillaume said:

"I couldn't care less about the mayor's daughter."

César was touched by this ardour:

"We'll see, son, we'll see. Go home now, it's getting late. Farewell!"

Guillaume said goodbye with a son's tenderness.

"God bless you, César!"

He left without looking back. César lost sight of him very quickly, and soon the lantern followed the turn in the path; so he went back into the house. Angelina was looking towards the door, as if in anticipation.

"The doctor's gone?"

She added, with an attempt at levity:

"Without saying goodbye?"

"It's late. I told him to get going."

"He could have eaten with us – I've made a nice stew of your rabbit."

"He'll come another time, love."

Sitting in his armchair beside the fire, César took out his tobacco pouch and calmly filled his pipe, then chose a fine piece of cherry wood from the log pile and, opening his penknife, began to whittle the wood.

Angelina made herself busy stirring casseroles.

"It's almost as if," she said finally, "you don't like him coming to visit us…"

Jean, sitting in his place at the table that had been laid for dinner, looked up from his newspaper.

"You, on the other hand," he said, "like it an awful lot."

Angelina shrugged, trying to extricate herself with dignity from her brother's mockery:

"He's a good man, always ready to help others, and his visits are an honour… That's all."

This was more or less what Célestine declared, loudly, when the doctor came home:

"You do them a great honour by going up to see them. You really have no idea."

"No, I really don't, Célestine."

Guillaume hung up his coat in the entrance and pulled off his fur-lined boots. He continued to pay no attention to his housekeeper, who was in a foul mood. She attempted to disguise it by talking about his supper:

"It's so late! If it had been a patient, I'd make nothing of it."

Her tone sharpened:

"It's true! If I asked you to go up there, it was for the lad, because they're quite capable of letting him run about with wild beasts! It wasn't to fall in love with that girl!"

Guillaume was patient: Célestine had looked after his mother during her last illness, and had tended to her devotedly. He took his instruments out of his bag and checked them. Emboldened by this silence, Célestine continued:

"Ha! You say nothing – you can't say I'm wrong: you spent the whole day there… well, more or less! It wasn't four o'clock when you left! Any longer and I was going to send for you, and then we'd have seen what we'd have seen!"

Carried away by her emotions, she was not weighing her words carefully.

"Would it hurt you to keep your mouth shut, Célestine?"

"Mouth shut!" exclaimed the housekeeper, ignoring Guillaume's furious look. "Mouth shut? It's my duty to warn you! I don't miss a thing now, do I? I can see her making eyes at you, the cunning minx! And what is she at the end of the day? A basket-seller, nothing more! Whereas the mayor's daughter…"

The exasperated tone of his reply astonished her:

"Not again!"

"What do you mean, 'not again'? I've never said a word about it."

"No," replied Guillaume, master of himself once more, "no, but César just did."

This threw her:

"Well! That proves he's not so daft, the old man. He knows perfectly well that you're not right for his Angelina."

"Enough, Célestine," scolded the doctor. "I forbid you to say her name."

Moreover, in his rage, he added:

"You're nothing but an old magpie!"

"Oh!" gasped Célestine.

She repeated "An old magpie!" with a hiccup, and whimpered, on the edge of tears:

"No one's ever said such a thing to me..."

She went on to list:

"Fifteen years of service with your grandmother, three with your mother, the poor saint..."

Breathing with effort, she managed to calm herself and carry on in a dignified manner:

"It doesn't matter... It only proves that things are worse than I feared. Listen to me, Doctor: I have my opinions and nothing you can say will change them. If your poor mother were still with us, she would agree with me! She... she used to say to me, "He'll be a doctor, Célestine... He'll make a good marriage..."

Guillaume cut in harshly:

"It's not just me – it takes two to marry. Who's talking about marriage?"

Célestine breathed in: things were not as terrible as she had supposed.

"Well! Nobody, fortunately!"

Sneakily, she turned the conversation around:

"It's just, you see, that I know how to look ahead! One day, let me tell you, little Sébastien will be devoured by that ferocious beast and you'll be bawling your eyes out."

With the help of her rich imagination, she pictured the dramatic scene. Carried away by her eloquence, she returned to her main theme, forgetting her wise attempt at caution:

"And do you not think she could keep an eye on him, instead of chasing after you? If I don't get involved, we'll soon see that cunning An... well, you know who... all in white and hanging from your arm. Now that," she cried out suddenly with a great theatrical gesture, "I could never bear. Never... Oh no!"

Icily, Guillaume warned her:

"Careful, Célestine: you're going too far."

"Fine!..." Célestine conceded.

With Provençal caution coming to her aide, she managed to control her emotions:

"Fine!... Well now, come and eat and let's hear no more about it."

Nonetheless, charging into her kitchen, she continued to grumble loudly enough for the doctor to hear:

"Maybe I'm not allowed to speak out, but I can at least serve dinner... Holy Mother of God! The things I have to put up with!"

She lifted a pot lid and addressed her personal opinion to the soup:

"When you consider the mayor's daughter is fetching and educated and everything! Ah well!"

The soup was transferred into the tureen and, majestically, Célestine came and deposited the tureen on the table, in front of Guillaume, who appeared to be absorbed in reading the newspaper. How weak men are!

Célestine preferred to resume hostilities from another angle:

"And with all the time you spent there, I suppose César has at least been warned? He's going to take care of the boy... And rid the countryside of that beast?"

He made no reply. With the newspaper open in front of him, he pretended to read in order to get some peace. Célestine truly was exhausting! The Beast, the Beast... What was the matter with everyone, that all they could talk about was that animal?

At the same moment, in the house on the mountain, the Beast was also the topic of conversation.

When the meal was finished, Jean had gone upstairs to sleep after helping Angelina tidy the dishes: a silent Angelina lost in her own thoughts. She had undressed Sébastien, and was now busy preparing the lanterns for each of them.

César, sitting beside the fire, was still whittling the piece of wood. Sitting at his feet, Sébastien was watching the work:

"I know," he said. "You're making a sculpture of Belle!"

"That's right," admitted César. "You guessed it."

"But," Sébastien resumed after a moment, "you've never seen her, have you?"

The old man smiled with his eyes:

"What do you know about it, Sébastien?"

His thumb trimmed and polished the piece.

"When I've finished," he continued, "you'll hang this yourself above our door. Then the Beast will understand. She will know that she is welcome here and she will come. This is how, in the old days, our forefathers defended themselves against wolves… They say that, often, the most ferocious of them recognized the sign, and they came and ate out of the children's hands, without fear or loathing… She will come!"

As he crouched at César's feet, the fire picked up a seam of light in Sébastien's hair… Sébastien who was daydreaming as he watched the flames, a faint smile on his lips.

4

The following day, in the frozen dawn, Belle came down to the village. The clock tower had just struck eight, it was still completely dark, but already doors and windows could be heard opening: the children were heading off to school.

Belle had stopped at the entrance to the village. Water dripped slowly along an icicle on the broken gutter of the Daniéli family house, each drop making a black hole in the snow that covered a wooden tub. Belle was listening.

Close by, she heard the sound of small clogs running along the paving stones of the lane. They faded away towards the square and silence returned, troubled only by the almost inaudible sound of those water drops hitting the black hole in the snow of the tub.

She moved on, turned at the corner of Sidonie's shop and crossed the square where the market was held every Saturday. The great plane trees watched, unmoved and indifferent, as she skirted round the church.

In front of her, to the right, the butcher's shop assistant was raising the metal shutters. He went quickly back into the lit-up shop and began to prepare the day's orders. Belle stopped and sniffed. The sound of a shutter banging made her run. She growled as she passed in front of the kennel that belonged to Martial, the mayor's dog, who guarded the only (and useless) railings of the village: railings that, although they served no purpose, had been erected here because they made the house stand out from the others, in this Provençal village where the houses stand tall and straight and all in a line. Because this house was set a metre behind the others, the opportunity had been taken to install these modern railings, which had cost a pretty penny!

Martial, scenting Belle, made an almost unbelievable noise amid the silence of the snow. A voice told him to be quiet. Belle growled quietly, making Martial retreat, warily, to the back of his kennel.

It was not yet daylight, but the night was brightening, and shadows began to emerge from the houses. One of these shadows glimpsed Belle. It returned in a hurry to the house, crying out:

"The Beast! The Beast! I've seen it!"

A window opened in the façade of the neighbour's house. A man's head emerged, his chin covered in shaving foam.

"Where? Where have you seen the Beast?"

He did not intend to listen to the answer: without pausing to wipe his chin, the man had already seized his gun and, holding it in one hand, was trying to shrug on his coat. He was in the street before the woman had finished her story:

"...and then I saw it take off towards the square! Oh, Holy Mother!"

She called all of the windows that were opening as her witnesses:

"Mother of Christ, pray for us... Hey, what do you think you're up to? You're a menace!"

She said this to her neighbour who was brandishing his gun.

"I'm going to shoot it, by God!" he explained. "But where is the damned thing?"

A child's voice cried out. Another voice, the mother's, sounded above the din:

"What is all this noise? Now the little one's awake!"

"The Beast... the Beast!"

It came from all over; it was as if the stones of the houses were talking, muttering or shouting tirelessly in almost supernatural terror, as if Belle, instead of being a large dog, lonely and possibly famished, had turned into the Dragon, the Tarasque – in short, Evil itself, which the saints in ancient times had bound in chains. However, the only one who thought this was old Roselyne – old Roselyne who, each morning, lit the candle in front of the statue of St Martha walking her Tarasque as one might a puppy, on the end of a ribbon. The others preferred a gun to the ribbon of a saint! The ancient urge to kill, so entrenched in the hearts of men, had woken up. In their minds, Belle had to become an evil beast, so that she could be hunted down for the common good, so that at last there might be general rejoicing: the great mountain hunt.

Belle, meanwhile, found herself suddenly presented with an incredible opportunity: the butcher's shop was right in front of her, full of quarters of meat and almost empty of people! The dog sniffed, her nose against the glass, and – oh, what a miracle! – this pressure was enough to open the door of the shop.

You can guess what happened: grabbing a leg of lamb with open jaws, then escaping in full view of the assistant who was returning from the back room – two actions so swift that this assistant, although he armed himself with the nearest thing that came to hand and chased after the thief, crying "Thief! The Beast! The Beast!", found Belle already far away, racing towards the mountain, where her white fur soon blended into the snow and the paleness of the coming day.

It was like a signal. In record time, the whole countryside was up to speed, but the news, as it spread from mouth to mouth, took on absurd proportions: legitimate worry, the primal thrill of the chase and that collective madness that takes hold of crowds, all told against Belle. So much so that the sexton did not hesitate to ring the alarm bell. As a result, the whole village turned out on the square! Henceforth, the hunting of "the Beast", which until this point had been just one of those vague plans that people talk about without intending to do anything, became, in almost everybody's mind, a necessity.

"What we have to do is save the countryside," lamented Ricard, the saddler, whom no one had ever heard say so much, given that ordinarily his wife did the talking for him.

Nothing less!

Naturally, Célestine took up a prominent place in this crusade, and it was thanks to her that people told as many stories about Belle as they did about the Dahu or the Paradine Beast. Rose Boudu, in a fit of maternal sentiment, affirmed that nothing would persuade her to send her children to school so long as the Beast was alive. To which Victorine added that "it ate an entire side of beef" in the butcher's shop.

Hearing this, Célestine decided to collect her meat order herself. It went against her principles, but to hell with dignity! She had to know.

The butcher's shop was full of customers, and the boss, like his assistant, did not know where to turn.

"A little patience, ladies – everyone will be served…"

Célestine cornered the poor man beside the weighing scales:

"As for me," she said, "I'll have a nice piece of tenderloin."

The butcher, who was weighing cutlets for the mayor, instructed his assistant:

"Go and see if we have any left."

"You ordered it yesterday, Madame Célestine: it's ready for you," said the innocent.

Célestine eyed him:

"Well, my boy… What if I want some more? Is that any of your business?"

"Come on, go," said the butcher.

The assistant resisted the urge to roll his eyes. However, Célestine had the art of sugaring every pill.

"I must say, he is brave, that lad," she cried at full volume.

"You can say that again – and modest! Oh, he's so modest! He hardly talks about it and, to hear him tell it, the Beast just came and went, like that… as it pleased – so he didn't even have time to catch his breath!"

The hero of the day returned from the cold room with a piece of beef in his hand.

"I said it from the start," resumed Célestine. "A dangerous animal must be hunted down and shot!"

When her meat had been weighed, she walked with her gendarme's gait to where the proprietress was shivering in the glass cage of the till, and handed her a hundred-franc note. As she gave back the change, the butcher's wife flattered her valued customer:

"You can say that again, Madame Célestine – that animal is a menace! It makes me shiver to think it comes down to the village! Would you believe it – a six-pound leg of lamb! What if it had been a child?"

Célestine took her time, carefully folding her banknotes, listening to the general conversation, ready to throw the weight of her personal opinion into the discussion. The shop was full to the rafters – all the gossips were there, and she knew very well that the women's determination would push the men towards the mountain.

Now, if you should ask me why Célestine so peculiarly detested Belle, I would say that I have no idea. The best I could do would be to suggest that the good woman liked to make trouble in the village for the pleasure of having her own importance confirmed to her.

The chorus of women rehearsed the dangers posed by Belle's presence. All the saints dear to the people of Provence were invoked.

"An animal of such a size, Holy Mother!"

"With jaws so terrible even St Martha would have been afraid of it!"

"My Antoine would have got it – only little Victor got between the gun and the Beast... Mother of Christ! He only just missed!"

Appalled, Victorine asked:

"Who? The little one?"

"Goodness, no! The Beast, I mean!"

Célestine weighed in, making the first sensible comment:

"It's for the municipal council to decide."

Having said this, she crossed the shop and glared at the butcher on her way out. Being a municipal councillor himself, he took this to heart. He rescued himself with a sideways attack:

"Is that the doctor's opinion, Madame Célestine? Because for the council, that would be moral support—"

"Well, naturally," concluded Célestine, without compromising herself.

And with these words, she made an impressive exit.

Meanwhile, up at the house, Belle was also the main of topic of conversation, though for a very different reason. César, applying himself to Sébastien's wishes, was using his knowledge, both of animals and of the old legends that have run in the mountains of Provence since time immemorial, to persuade Belle to accept the child's friendship. It was for this reason that the old man, standing on a stepladder, was hanging above the door the statuette of the dog, the "sign" that he had sculpted the previous evening.

Sébastien's cheerful spirits were not entirely satisfied:

"You think she'll understand?"

With a mouth full of nails, César found it difficult to answer:

"Yep... she'll understand."

"And the sign – what if she doesn't see it?"

César took the nails out of his mouth, one by one, and hammered them in with little blows.

"Then she'll smell the lard you've put out in the little bowl."

This explanation was satisfactory. All of a sudden, Sébastien was full of enthusiasm:

"Where shall I put the bowl? Do you think it'll work here?"

"It would be better a bit farther away... The dog won't be at ease that close to the door."

Sébastien came down the stone staircase as steep as a ladder. This took time and courage: carrying a bowl full of bread dipped in lard, without looking down at his feet, was risky! Having at last put down his burden, Sébastien peered up at César: he was attaching the "sign" to a length of chain before hanging it from the nails hammered into the pediment of the door. It was pretty and very visible; there was reason to hope that Belle would notice it. As for the bowl, which Angelina had given him, it was full of perfectly delicious things.

Sébastien, with knitted eyebrows and his nose in the air, persisted:

"So do you think she'll come?"

César came down the stepladder and sat on the lowest wrung. He took time again to light his pipe.

"Nobody," he said at last, "can live on their own for ever. She will come to us because this is the most isolated house, and she will be your friend if you want it... By which I mean, if you love her."

Sébastien looked at the mountain: it was white all over, lit by the sun, with immense blue shadows here and there.

"And what if she doesn't come?"

He was worried, all of a sudden.

"You'll go out to her, and I'll come with you… You'll talk to her."

"What if she doesn't understand?"

"You'll try again."

"Yes," Sébastien said, with a huge sigh, "but it might take a long time… a very long time!"

He no longer looked towards the mountain but at César's pipe as he puffed away, making smoke rings that drifted and dissolved above their heads.

"It will take a long time," said the old man, "or no time at all… Who can say?"

He got up, took the stepladder and returned it to its place farther under the canopy.

"So goes the world that never wears out," he concluded.

Angelina opened the door:

"Lunchtime!"

She followed Sébastien's gaze towards the "sign".

"Oh," she said, "how pretty!"

"It's for Belle," Sébastien explained. "Do you think she'll come?"

The young woman concealed the tenderness in her laugh with humour:

"You've asked me so often, I can't tell any more!"

"I'm sure of it," said César.

Sébastien gave one of those smiles that lit up the world.

"Right then, let's eat!"

No sooner had César uttered these words than a call rang out:

"Hey! César… Ho!"

They turned towards the path where two men were walking, both of them armed.

"Hello," said Angelina, "visitors! What do Georges and Moulin senior want with us?"

The two men stopped at the bottom of the steps.

"Fetch your gun, César, and come with us: the mad dog attacked Moulin this morning, we're on its trail… It's not far off."

Angelina restrained Sébastien with a firm hand. César replied very calmly:

"If I take up my gun, it won't be against that animal, but against the men who are hunting her."

"D'you hear that, Georges," said Moulin senior, laughing aloud. "Ah, César! Always the joker!"

"I'm glad I amuse you," said the old man, "but I've said what I have to say."

The two men at the bottom of the steps were speechless for a moment. Then fury stole across their features. Georges was the first to express their feelings:

"Do you realize what you've just said?"

César, perfectly calm, asked sarcastically:

"Are you injured, Moulin?"

"No," the man conceded, "but I might well have been."

Then, in the fanciful Provençal manner, they described the misdeeds of Belle: she had frightened Moulin's horse as it carted a trailer loaded with wood, and then she had gone down to the village – nobody would deny it! Ten… a hundred people had seen her devouring a lamb in the butcher's shop! The assistant had done his best to fight back, but what can you do against such a monster? Now she was near the house, they were sure of it, and that was why they had come, ahead of the beat planned for tomorrow.

"And so, like Georges said, we took our guns and came up to ask for your help, César…"

"Because you're a good shot! We're sure to get her if you're with us."

"Just think of the rabies she might give someone if she bites them!"

"That animal's healthy," said César. "She doesn't have rabies."

He called out placidly:

"Angelina… Bring me my gun."

"Ah," sighed Georges, "you're making your mind up finally."

César, strangely calm, replied in a low voice:

"If I load my gun, it won't be against that poor homeless dog…"

Moulin senior thought he might choke with rage:

"Can I tell you something, César? With all due respect, you're an old lunatic!"

Sébastien ran down the stairs at breakneck speed.

"Sébastien!" cried Angelina.

However, the lad stood before Moulin, fists raised:

"And *you*, you're a liar!"

A well-aimed kick sent him sprawling on the ground, and Georges, beside himself with rage, bellowed:

"You, gypsy, I'd advise you to keep your mouth shut!"

Then César, his jaw set, addressed the two men, who sensed from the way he spoke that he would brook no argument:

"Now, the first person who touches this child or who fires at that dog I will consider fair game… Go to the village and tell that to everyone! Consider that my warning to you!"

Angelina had rushed up and, with her hands on the boy's shoulders, stared at the two men with flashes of rage in her eyes. This did not prevent Georges from answering back:

"All the same, we'll have the hide of your filthy animal, whether you like it or not."

Sébastien tightened his fists, and Angelina did not have time to restrain him. Violently, the boy had broken free and was running with all his strength towards the mountain. Angelina cried out in distress:

"Sébastien! Sébastien, come back!"

Just as she was about to run after him, her grandfather's hand held her back:

"Let him go. It isn't the first time he has run about the mountain. It's how boys become men in these parts."

"But... the Beast!"

"I know what I know. That animal is neither rabid nor dangerous. He's got nothing to fear... him even less than anyone else."

Georges and Moulin had decided to make themselves scarce. César did not even look at them; he pushed Angelina towards the house with a gesture that was both firm and gentle.

"Come on, lass, I'm hungry. You can keep Sébastien's share... He'll be back this evening."

Sébastien was struggling in the soft snow. Instinctively, without even thinking about the way, he was heading towards the Baou. All around him, the great moraine was changing into a fantastical scenery of fallen rocks and pinnacles. The silence seemed infinite; the little figure in the midst of it seemed unconnected to human society. He was, undoubtedly, not contemplating any of this. He walked, and from time to time

he cupped his two hands in front of his mouth and called out:

"Belle!"

Then he gave a longer cry, which the echo repeated. And Belle heard it. Now she in turn walked towards him. Was it the age-old instinct of her ancestors, the great rescue dogs? She travelled towards those cries that summoned her at regular intervals. With her strong and steady gait, she skirted round the customs post, keeping her distance. Near the refuge, she hesitated. However, since she knew without needing to understand, she did not take the Grand Défilé, where the vast rocks pile up, a chaotic muddle, near-eternal witnesses to the rage of the mountain. Several times she sank into the snow. Pushing with her hind legs, she was on the move again, and so it went on until she came to the big black cross. It was then, emerging from one of the rocky corridors, that Sébastien saw her.

Motionless and waiting, she stood on her four powerful legs, watching him.

He wanted to run to catch up with her, but his strength gave out, and the poor little human creature subsided into the snow, sobbing with cold and hunger and exhaustion.

It was at this moment that a dog's passion for man was truly born in Belle. In a few agile bounds she was next to him, lifting him with her muzzle, breathing her strength into the child, forcing him to hang on to the long frozen locks of her fur. Sébastien still sobbed, but for joy now. She, for her part, stepped back when she felt his strength return. However, she did not run away. She walked around him, tamping down the snow in a big circle. Sébastien could only say, repeatedly:

"Belle… My Belle… I'm your friend. You'll see, they won't hurt you. César promised!"

It was like a litany of love, tenderness and faith.

After lunch, Angelina had settled herself by the window and, with all her tools and her willow rods around her, had forgotten her worries. Things changed when she had finished the first basket. When she looked up at the clock for the first time, it was three o'clock, and though the daylight had not yet diminished, it was possible to see nightfall coming: the old and very beautiful copper sauce-pans, of which she was so proud, shone in the rays of the sun as they fell slantwise through the west window. César noticed his granddaughter's expression:

"Don't worry, lass…"

"I can't understand why you're not doing anything!"

Her worry was great enough to shake her confidence in her grandfather. He, for his part, smoked his pipe in little puffs. His face in profile did not flinch, and he made no reply. Angelina started on a difficult task: a basket braided with fine and flexible willow, following a particularly complicated design, and which she could never complete in one sitting. She set it down almost at once, too anxious to go on:

"Grandfather!"

Her voice trembled with genuine distress:

"Grandfather, it will be night soon!"

This time, he turned to look at her:

"Don't you worry, Angelina. If I didn't have my reasons, I'd go off to find him. But it has to be this way, do you see? Sébastien has to be on his own."

She implored him:

"But... the Beast?"

"Exactly," said César.

The day was ending now, very tenderly, with a milky light as of dawn, though the great black shadows of the summits were spreading terribly fast across the snow. Angelina went away from the window, unable any longer to watch them gaining inexorably on the last swathes of brightness.

She carried her work to the hearth beside César. He had been busying himself since lunchtime with little tasks. In fact, chiefly, he had been smoking, and by this unusual behaviour Angelina understood that he was preoccupied. She said nothing more: it was pointless – he would stay silent, even if he were as worried as she was. She got up briskly, went towards the door and opened it: the footsteps she had just heard belonged to Jean, who was coming back from work. She muttered:

"I was hoping it would be Sébastien..."

He stopped, alarmed:

"He isn't back? How long has he been gone?"

"It was well before noon – he hasn't even eaten."

"Sometimes I really don't understand you," the young man grumbled.

This was aimed much more at his grandfather than at Angelina. César lifted his eyebrows and Jean, cowed by this look, added quickly:

"No doubt you have your reasons, Grandfather, but it's night-time now. And the kid's only six… I'm going!"

Jean was putting on the hat that he had taken off when he came in. César was about to give an order… but there was no need. Sébastien came into the house. His eyes blinked in the light; he looked exhausted. His gaze travelled from one of them to another, a sleepwalker's gaze, as if he did not see them, as if they were transparent and he had seen something else entirely through them.

"What time do you call this to be coming home?" scolded Jean.

But Sébastien was walking towards César. He stopped in front of the old man and told him solemnly:

"I've spoken to her…"

César gave him back his solemn look, then nodded his head, and a glimmer of a smile softened his wrinkled old face. He was proud of Sébastien.

"Go and sleep... She will have need of you tomorrow."

With his face still turned towards an inner vision, the child walked up to his bed under the stairs. He fell into it fully dressed. Angelina quite forgot to feed him. And Sébastien, to avoid questions perhaps, closed his eyes.

Tomorrow, he would go to find Belle... tomorrow, and all the days until the day she finally decided to enter the house.

"He's worn out... We shouldn't allow it," said Angelina.

She did not dare look at her grandfather, but it was obvious that she was full of reproaches.

Jean was cheerful again and warmed his hands by the fire.

"Everything will be better tomorrow..."

Tomorrow... tomorrow. All of them had no other word in their mouths.

"Tomorrow," said the mayor, "the men will assemble at seven o'clock in front of the school. We will be up there between eight and nine o'clock and, with a bit of luck, we will have rid the mountain of that damned beast by midday..."

He was sitting with the butcher beside a low table in the doctor's living room. It was the end of the day. Célestine was serving drinks, and since she intended to listen in, she devoted herself to pointless business between her cupboards and the table. After this, she busied herself with the fire, arranging the logs, pushing at the ashes. She cast glances at the doctor. He was toying absent-mindedly with his glass.

"César," he said, "thinks we should leave the animal be... and when César has a notion, we'd do well to respect it."

The butcher had no time for this nonsense.

"Moulin and Georges told the meeting all about that. Poor César was a remarkable man in his time, but he's old... too old!"

He looked at the mayor, who was smiling pityingly. Célestine did not dare join the conversation – though not for want of enthusiasm – but she approved of it with her eyes.

"I wouldn't mind having his knowledge of the natural world," said the doctor sharply. "Old or not, he's a man of feeling and a man of experience. I've always followed his advice and always come out well of it."

The butcher cut through difficulties as easily as he cut through his meats:

"In other words, Doctor, we shouldn't rely on you for the hunt tomorrow?"

"No," said Guillaume.

This was short and to the point.

"Very well!"

The butcher emptied his glass and stood up irritably.

"Why," added Guillaume, trying to be conciliatory, "should we treat a dog like a wild animal? It's a bit ridiculous. Let her take her chances!"

The butcher remarked that the dog was no doubt struggling to find food on the mountain. "So when she comes into my shop, I don't find that terribly funny!"

The mayor was mollifying:

"I understand. By God, it's no laughing matter!"

Then he said to the doctor:

"Think about it, Doctor... Opinion in Saint-Martin is unanimous: people will not understand why you've gone against it. Besides, we need good shots, and you've no equal when it comes to hunting, apart from César – but as for him... So, what about it – tomorrow, seven o'clock, with your gun... Don't answer now, just sleep on it!"

Guillaume took the mayor's proffered hand but shook his head:

"My mind is made up. Goodnight, Monsieur the Mayor. I won't wish you good hunting."

Thus, Belle's fate appeared sealed, alone in her lofty solitude against all those guns. Alone with Sébastien as her friend.

But also with César's protection.

It was still dark the next morning when the men of the village gathered in the square, all of them carrying guns.

The mayor was among the last to arrive and the doctor was with him.

"Eh," bellowed the butcher, "I knew he'd see sense if he slept on it."

"No," said Guillaume, "I'm not coming with you. I've a patient to see in Notre-Dame-de-la-Menour."

Enthusiasm dwindled, especially when he added: "I don't like dog-hunting."

It was impossible to hold his comments against him. His devotion inspired respect. They watched him take off, with his bag on his back, towards the high mountain pasture where old Tonelli kept his flock in a sheepfold that was almost impossible to see, so closely did its low roofs of flat stone resemble the rocks. It was more than an hour's walk away, and no car could get up there. Everyone knew that the old man was ill and that Guillaume was trying to persuade him to admit himself to hospital.

"Old folk," said Grandfather Moulin, who was eighty-three years young, "are stubborn sometimes! He'd be better off in town, nice and warm in hospital... but you try persuading the old crackpot!"

And Guillaume went up to La Menour twice a week to treat the old shepherd himself. If he did not want to hunt a dog, how could they resent him for it?

The butcher spoke aloud what everyone was thinking:

"It's that old lunatic César who's stuffed his head with nonsense – otherwise he'd be with us."

They began to walk towards the Baou, since Moulin claimed to have encountered Belle that way. They took the short cut and Angelina saw them from far away as they climbed, a procession of tiny ants in the vast snowfield.

She hurried towards the village and the doctor's house.

Célestine, who opened the door, was disinclined to be friendly: the doctor's refusal to participate in the beat had been a failure of her diplomacy. She put all the blame on César.

"Ah, so there you are," she said. "We haven't seen you for a long time."

Angelina skipped the formalities:

"I'm here to see the doctor."

"You don't say!" mocked Célestine. "I don't expect you came here to see me!"

But Angelina was in a hurry:

"I must talk to him… He's the only one who can sort things out with my grandfather."

This made the gossip in Célestine salivate:

"Ah! Now what's happening?"

Angelina, as already mentioned, was in a hurry, and ill disposed to give things away:

"He's the one I'll tell."

"Very well," said Célestine angrily. "Unfortunately, he's not in."

"Where is he?"

Célestine relished her revenge:

"What business is that of yours, my pretty?"

"Madame Célestine," the girl stammered, "for pity's sake…"

Out of the question! When it came to Angelina, Célestine was made of stone.

"Shall I tell you what I think? Well, if I were in your position, I would be ashamed… ashamed to run after a man who's too good for you!"

The large, clear eyes stared at the housekeeper: Angelina had not yet understood.

"That's it, go on, play the innocent. Think I'm blind, do you? I was young once!"

"You'd never believe it!" replied Angelina fiercely.

And she set off at a run because her tears were starting to flow, and she wanted to conceal them from Célestine, who let fly her last, and cruellest, arrow:

"Just you wait for the mayor's daughter to come back… You'll see if he has eyes for you then!"

Angelina came to a halt. Upon which Célestine's voice took on a honeyed tone:

"Everyone's talking about the two of them getting married – didn't you know?"

By the time Angelina had to stop running because she could no longer put off blowing her nose, and because she realized that she had lost all dignity, she was at the edge of the village, in front of Sidonie, who had a bundle of dried herbs on her head.

"Well now, lass, where are you running to like that? Tell me, what's the matter?"

Angelina hurriedly concealed her handkerchief, but she had no way of hiding her red eyes.

"Nothing," she said. "I'm looking for the doctor."

"Lord Jesus!" exclaimed the good woman. "And is that a reason for crying?"

"Of course not," snapped Angelina.

"Yes, but… Oh, Holy Mother! Is someone ill at yours? It's not the little one, is it? Or your grandfather? It can't be Jean: I saw him going off to work…"

She stopped guessing for the simple reason that there was no one else to mention, but (as she confided in Victorine five minutes later) her kind heart was "all turned over".

Angelina, aware all of a sudden that her manner was going to be the source of endless gossip, exploded:

"It's me, obviously!"

Sidonie was not stupid! There were things, even, that she understood very well.

"Right. I see," she conceded. "It's none of my business... even so, listen: I heard the doctor say that he was off to see a patient over towards La Menour. It must be old Tonelli. So if you go quickly, you'll find him!"

"Thank you, Madame Sidonie," cried Angelina, and her step bore a striking resemblance to that of her goat when it yearns in spring to gambol on the fresh mountain grass.

Sidonie smiled kindly:

"Eh! Young folk, how they run!"

Then, having a sudden thought, she shouted loudly:

"Wait for him at the chapel, lass – you can't miss him!"

Of course! At the chapel of Notre-Dame!

Angelina got there in record time. She crossed the footbridge by which pious pilgrims had in days gone by made the abyss passable. Ever since, this route had been maintained, for Notre-Dame-de-la-Menour was both a place of devotion and a tourist spot for the region. Angelina waited there, sitting on the stone step, convinced that she would see Guillaume, wherever he came from, in the vast landscape that she could see stretching out at her feet.

Suddenly, she saw him. She jumped up and crossed the footbridge. He saw her running towards him.

"Angelina... Have you been looking for me?"

A little out of breath, she said very quickly:

"Yes... You have to go up towards the Baou, at once!"

She implored him:

"I know that you have your patients, but... he went up there at sunrise, with his gun!"

"César?"

"Yes. He had that grumpy expression of his. And he let Sébastien go ahead of him... all on his own! And it wasn't yet daylight. I wanted to keep him back, so he said to me, 'Don't be frightened: he's got nothing to fear up there.' But the worst thing was, he added that, between them and him, there was his gun! You have to talk to him! You're the only one who can make him see sense."

He took her bare hand and, gently, kissed its palm. He spoke to her as to a child:

"It's too late, little one. They've been gone since dawn – they can't be far from the Baou..."

Suddenly ferocious, she remembered the words of Célestine:

"So you can't do anything?"

She pulled back her hand as if something in Guillaume's was burning her.

"If I'd known, I wouldn't have come to find you. Célestine wouldn't have been able to say a word to me!"

She tried to get away, but he, suddenly as fierce as her, had seized hold of her arms:

"What are you talking about? Was she rude to you?"

"No, it's nothing. Let me go."

"What did she say to you, Angelina? You have every right – she's got nothing to say to you! Do you understand?"

He sensed that she was no longer trying to get away.

"Don't worry about César: he knows what he's doing. He has more experience than all of us."

She was happy to be at his side, as if his presence alone protected her from all the dark thoughts that had troubled her.

"Doctor… You don't think he's going mad?"

He laughed with that laugh she loved, that reminded her of his real age and brought him closer to her.

"Your grandfather? Ah, don't you believe it!"

And yet, what would she have thought if she could have seen César at that instant, standing on the rocky ridge above the Petit Défilé, César who, with his gun in his hand, calmly awaited the troop of men who were coming up towards the Baou, in order to block their route.

A little farther down, they had stopped in their tracks. No matter how edgy the beat made them, and they anticipated an enjoyable day of it, even the most excited stood motionless. The mayor spoke aloud the gnawing worry felt by all:

"The old fool's quite capable of shooting at us."

"You're the mayor, aren't you?" cried George. "Go talk sense into him!"

The mayor could not go backwards, so he went forwards:

"Hey! Up there! César... Ho!"

When he was closer, he spoke severely:

"This business could end badly for you..."

César, with an expression of perfect calm, cocked his weapon: the action, visible to everyone, caused a low murmur, but nobody spoke. When silence returned, everyone listened to César:

"Whoever kills an innocent does not deserve to live... Lay down your guns and follow me: I'll prove to you that big dog would bring happiness to any household."

It would be too much to pretend that they wanted to obey, yet the old man's gun never missed its target, it was a sure thing, and... who knew what he was capable of in a moment of anger? Georges, who remembered having called him an old lunatic, was the first to favour an amicable solution.

"Listen, César, since you insist, prove to us whatever you want."

In resignation, the mayor disarmed his rifle, and everyone else did likewise. César slung his own over his shoulder and took the head of the column.

They were not far from the dry stone refuge, at the spot where for nearly seven years the big mournful cross had stood, when they saw the child. He was playing with the white dog. Around them, in the silence of the snow, the vast white landscape stretched out as if asleep in the quiet of a fine afternoon. The sun made the summits of the Demoiselle and the Baou gleam, as it did the crescent-shaped ridge that marked the frontier between them.

Speaking softly, the butcher asked:

"Wasn't it there, in the refuge, that the lad was born?"

César, without taking his eyes off the child and the dog as they played on their own, gave a nod of the head. Then the mayor regained his authority, but he too spoke quietly:

"You have to take that child home, César... and right away. It's madness to leave him all alone on the heights at this time of year!"

César did not look at him as he replied:

"He's not all alone..."

He gave a hand signal to go back down. The whole company obeyed him without a word. He turned around and looked, beyond the enormous cirque, at the summits that Belle would one day have to leave in order to follow Sébastien. When? No one could say. The dog had a long way to go before she rediscovered a love of people. Deep in her instinctive memory, the behaviour of the first animal to become a dog needed reviving; that unique gesture of the only wild creature to become tame of its own free will. This ancient, so ancient history was written in Belle, but certain men had caused her to forget it. Now, slowly, she was going to decipher it again. César looked from Sébastien to Belle – the Beast – and back to the child, each as pure as the other. From here on, he could do nothing more for them. Sébastien had made his choice: it was up to Belle to accept it or opt instead for the solitary freedom of the summits.

Old César went down among the villagers – who were surprised and moved, without knowing why, in the deepest part of themselves – and said once more:

"Those two have been looking for each other for a long time."

Silently, the men withdrew.

"You'll see," Sébastien was telling Belle. "It's nice at the house, it's warm, there are lots of good things to eat! And then we'll have Angelina and Jean and César to defend us, always… You'll come, Belle."

Moreover, it was not a child's promise, but a genuine commitment when he said to her:

"I'll wait for you."

He went away without looking back, and the big dog followed him. She followed him until the last swell of the moraine. From there the house was visible, far away and so small that it was scarcely possible to see the blue smoke rising from the fireplace where Angelina had just put a large log of oak. And it was impossible to make out the "sign" crafted by César, which trembled on the end of its chain, shaken by a breath of wind.

"Belle… I'll come back tomorrow… and every other day!"

She watched him go away, disappearing behind bends in the terrain, reappearing, disappearing again and finally walking up the steps of the house. There he turned: the place where he had left Belle was empty, but he could hear long and happy barking.

5

Every day, he went back to the Baou. Angelina did not dare say anything. César thought it enough to explain:

"The boy's even safer with her than he is with me."

The old man had given up hunting near the Baou, and the whole family was waiting for the day when Belle would come and take her place in the household.

In the village too, people were waiting. They were sceptical. A few men had kept, hidden deep within themselves, the emotion that had seized hold of them at the sight of Belle playing with Sébastien, but the others did not want to believe it: they disliked a story that was like something out of the legends of old. And Célestine more than anyone!

Because nobody had taken her advice. For Belle to have the right to join up with Sébastien, the doctor's housekeeper would have had to have foreseen it. So now, she kept saying:

"You're mad… If she were a dog, a proper one, she would have followed him, not wandered back with the wild animals! It'll end badly, but no one wants to listen to me."

The more she repeated this, the more she came to believe it.

Célestine was not one of those women who notices deep and carefully concealed feelings. She lived according to a very simple understanding of reality. At least, this was what she claimed: did it make the slightest sense to let a child wander about all day on the mountain? A child of six! The foolish and disobedient desire to appropriate the Beast had lured him out there. A beast that was sure to devour him one of these days. Well then, one more reason to rid the countryside of it!

Armed with this flawless argument, Célestine set out on her crusade against Belle. Her second crusade! One after another, she tried her luck with the village gossips, knowing perfectly well that they, in turn, would talk sense into the men.

This tactic worked perfectly with Séraphie, the mayor's wife, and Séraphie persuaded her still-hesitant husband.

"You should write to the dog pound, you know. That's Madame Célestine's opinion… The whole village is saying that you're not doing your duty as mayor!"

"What do you want me to tell the people at the pound?"

Séraphie shook her head.

"Whatever you like: tell them the Beast is nearby, harmless enough on the surface, that we could return her to them, maybe, if they wanted. Tell them about little Sébastien too… but what do I know?"

The mayor heaved a sigh, burrowed into his arm-chair and calmly lit his pipe, which was a sure way to exasperate his wife.

"So? Are you going to write to them?"

The mayor tamped the tobacco down a little in his pipe.

"Yes," he said.

"About time," moaned Séraphie.

"Only," continued the mayor, "there's something you're forgetting. The pound gave its opinion to all the mayors of the region. Remember: 'The animal is dangerous: whoever sees it is authorized to shoot it.' That's why I hadn't made up my mind to write to them. The boy is happy with that dog, and yet, for their part, the people from the pound are authorizing anyone to destroy it!"

"Things have changed a lot since then," muttered Séraphie.

Nevertheless, she was no longer quite so certain that writing to the pound was the right thing to do.

The mayor, however, was certain. It was his duty, after all. He sent a letter giving a precise account of the facts. Yet for all that, in the village, debate continued; and this put the mayor in a very bad temper. He had done his duty, hadn't he? So what did they have to reproach him for?

As it happened, the village was divided on the matter. Célestine noticed with regret that some of her friends were impervious to reason. Victorine, for instance, had taken Sébastien's side, and gave him a packet of sweets as a sign of her support.

"If you show them to the Beast, she's sure to follow you… They're honey-and-cream flavour!"

In short, there were some who were tender-hearted, like old Roselyne, who lit a candle in front of the statue of St Martha walking her Tarasque on the end of a ribbon, or like the butcher's assistant (a sentimental soul) who always put a packet of scraps in Angelina's bag when she came down to buy meat.

"For the Beast," he would say.

Meanwhile, the butcher's wife was not in the habit of forgiving insults, and what insult, I ask you, could be more cruel than the theft of a leg of lamb?

As for Madame Daniéli, she never understood anything... because she was deaf.

And Sidonie? Oh, you could never tell with Sidonie! She was as simple-minded as a child, and believed all sorts of nonsense. The last person to speak was surely in the right. An old fool with a weathervane for a head that twisted about in the wind! So much for Sidonie.

This left the others. Rose Boudu was becoming sentimental about Sébastien:

"The little one doesn't have a mother!"

She cried about it.

"Ah, the poor thing!"

Yet she had a horror of the Beast: this dated back to that lunchtime when Michel had told them about his encounter with Belle. Since then, Rose's fertile imagination had so successfully created an image of a monster that she came to believe in it. This despite the fact that, several times, Hippolyte had attempted to get things straight:

"Eh! Rose, why do you talk about things you don't know anything about? It is true: she's handsome, big and strong, that animal... Even so, there's quite a difference between her and the Paradine Beast!"

His efforts were in vain! Rose Boudu trembled for all the children of the district in general, and for her own in particular. Belle had to be chased away as far as possible. She was, therefore, in Célestine's camp, though within limits.

In short, there were those who were for and those who were against, with, in the middle, naturally, the vast majority of timid souls who would side later on with the winning party, and who said "yes" while thinking "no", or the other way round.

It came close to becoming a political issue, and the mayor had to defend himself in front of the municipal council. Tempers were fraying; there was a risk that words would be spoken that could not be retracted. Fortunately, Hippolyte Boudu pacified the opposing camps by commenting:

"Whether it's a good or a bad thing, Monsieur the Mayor has written to the dog pound, the letter has been sent, and all we can do is wait."

Meanwhile, Sébastien's status with the gang of schoolboys had risen since Antoine had suggested:

"We won't say 'gypsy' to Sébastien any more! Because I wouldn't have dared go near that animal!"

They had no opportunity to demonstrate this form of admiration, for Sébastien never came down to the village. He spent his days in the mountains, and Angelina, always with the same deep sighs, filled his shoulder bag with supplies every morning and, after a kiss on his pink cheek, watched him from the doorstep as he took off towards the Baou. Belle, invisible, must have been waiting for him, since each day Angelina heard the same joyful barking. Thus, gradually, almost without realizing it, she came to be reassured. And César, when he was about, smiled with his eyes.

One day, when Sébastien awoke, fog had taken possession of the mountain. It was impossible to see two metres ahead, and Angelina refused to let him go. It was true that, in the house, because Angelina came and went, because she talked, stirring her cooking pots or reviving the fire in the great fireplace, everything was full of life, whereas as soon as you opened the door, the silence seized hold of you, the silence of the high mountains, the silence of this place without people. Ahead of you and behind you and on all sides, there was an opaque world, muffled and ever so small, since there were these four walls that enclosed you and made you dread what you would encounter on the other side. As a result, you wanted not to go out, and anxiety put its hand inside you and slowly closed around your heart.

Angelina pushed Sébastien towards the gentle warmth of the hearth and closed the door.

"Belle is waiting for me," said Sébastien.

Frightened? Yes, he was frightened of those shifting walls, but he had said exactly what he had to say: "Belle is waiting for me." Therefore, he had to go.

"Well then, she'll wait for you... or else..."

Angelina set down the kettle of boiling water that she was going to pour into the tub before saying:

"Who knows? Perhaps she'll come looking for you!"

"If she comes, will you let me go?"

She would have preferred not to answer, because if she said no, he would be there watching her, stubborn and mournful.

"Will you let me go? Will you?"

"Where's the risk?" wondered the young woman, so she replied:

"Fine... If she comes calling for you, I won't say no."

He sat on the stone step in front of the fireplace, and began his long wait. Such was his confidence that Angelina felt ashamed of herself for having said "yes" while thinking "no".

Having finished preparing the vegetables for the soup, she came and sat down at the table, where, on spread-out newspapers, she began to furbish the copper pots. Sébastien, leaning his back against one of the stone posts, watched the reddening embers. A log caught fire. Motionless, he became one with the dance of high bright flames and the glow of sparks. The clock kept up its continuous, intimate chatter. The embers collapsed, and he was surrounded by weightless stars that took off, sucked up towards the sky by the great black hole of the chimney. He did not allow himself to get distracted, because in his heart there was only Belle, and his mind had to trace the route she was taking to get to him. He watched the weightless stars take flight. Perhaps Belle saw them too. Perhaps their light pierced the layer of cotton wool through which she was running, white in that frozen whiteness.

Now he heard her breathing, there, under the door. Angelina, too, had heard. She got up and pressed herself against it. Motionless, she listened. He too had got up with a bound, but stood frozen, taken unawares by joy.

"You can open up... It's Belle."

However, from the doorway Angelina saw only the ghost of a dog running and disappearing, a shadow among shadows, and Sébastien rapidly vanishing, snatched up by the fog, with his hat and his red jumper creating, for an instant, a vivid stain on the whiteness. The little one's voice still reached her:

"You see, she came..."

And Sébastien's laugh clambered all the way to the porch and the "sign" that hung beneath it.

She ran, trying to catch up with him. It was impossible, however, in this fog that hid things and stifled all sounds.

Towards the east, the fog has finally given way to the rising sun, and now there is a brilliant, almost white light. The light pleases Sébastien, because it reveals the spruces along the bank of the Gordolasque and rids them of their menace. At the foot of these trees, the torrent glimmers, following its tortuous path through rocks that it must, at times, leap across. In so doing, it becomes an infinite number of waterfalls, and this is when it makes the true noise of a torrent – the booming that reverberates from the mountains as the wind carries it this way and that.

In certain places, where there is almost no slope, the water makes only a soft sound as it passes over the pebbles: a sound like silk when you rub it between your fingers. Sébastien can imitate it very well with the shawl that Angelina wears on holy days and on Sundays to go to Mass. Who could imagine that this stream, whose current turns slowly around tiny stones, is the very same Gordolasque as that of the gorge, below the Pas-du-Loup, the one that bellows more loudly than old Domingo's big red bull? Sébastien has crossed it twice using a fallen-down tree, but Belle prefers to jump it. Sébastien admires her strength. He could not have done it!

"Monsieur might put these things better than I can! I am a simple woman, Monsieur, and all I know is: that dog does not belong to Sébastien! And you know as well as I do, 'Thou shalt not steal...'"

Célestine called him "Monsieur" in order to show her displeasure. This was impossible to misinterpret – for Guillaume more than for anyone.

"Of course, Célestine."

He spread out his newspaper in front of him, propped it up against the wine bottle and pretended to be exceptionally interested in what he was reading. His only desire was to make his housekeeper understand that he hated her gossiping, her ill-informed judgements, and that he found the way she tried to run the show in the village unbearable.

"I take it Monsieur thinks as I do? That dog belongs to a pound, so it must go back... Does Monsieur want any more beef?"

"No thank you, Célestine."

"So, will Monsieur discuss it with César?"

"Célestine, you know perfectly well that the dog runs free on the mountain and that César can't do a thing about it, except shoot her as if she were game... which he will not do. As for bringing a corpse back to the pound... which I don't even know!"

"I have the address, Monsieur – I kept the newspaper."

Guillaume, exasperated, gave up on his reading.

"And even if you know the address, would you know how to catch the animal? With a lasso, perhaps? We're not in Texas, Célestine!"

Even sarcasm had no effect on the housekeeper.

"Monsieur is forgetting that the animal follows little Sébastien everywhere! I should think it would be easy—"

Guillaume cut in:

"Easy?"

"It seems to me that, if we really wanted to, we could catch it while it's playing with the boy. Georges saw them only yesterday, playing by the river. I've spoken to the mayor about it, and he agrees that it wouldn't be impossible."

Guillaume's appearance of calm fooled her.

"In short, you think, and so does the mayor, that Sébastien could serve as bait? And who, I wonder, among the inhabitants of Saint-Martin, will take on this delightful task?"

"Oh, no one from Saint-Martin, Monsieur. We'd only have to… I mean to say, we only have to inform the pound. They have specialized staff, apparently…"

Guillaume stood up with such force that his chair fell over. Taken aback by this violence, Célestine picked it up again.

"But Monsieur—"

"It's disgraceful, let me tell you – disgraceful. And that's putting it mildly! That child, Célestine, little Sébastien – but in a way, he should be everyone's child! He has no one to defend him, no one except for an old man and two children… and you would want to involve me in this outrage? Are you stupid, spiteful or thoughtless? The boy is a passionate, secretive being… He loves that animal and the animal loves him back. I don't know what he'd be capable of doing to keep her. Have you no heart, Célestine?"

"Indeed, Monsieur, and it's because I have a heart that I find it outrageous to let him go about the mountain all day long, on his own, with a dangerous animal. That's right, Monsieur, and your insults won't make any difference – a dangerous animal!"

Already Guillaume had stopped listening. He had put on his fur-lined jacket and his boots. The door slammed behind him.

Only when he was in front of the mayor's house did he regain his composure.

He went straight into the living room, practically knocking over Séraphie, who was shocked: the doctor, always so calm, so well brought-up, so full of good manners, was behaving in a way that Georges, the village drunkard, would not have dared. She trotted behind him.

Seeing this hurricane surging towards him, the mayor dropped his newspaper and stood up.

"To what do I owe the pleasure of?…"

"I've just been informed, Monsieur the Mayor," said the doctor, "that you think the big dog must be handed back to the pound where she came from, and that, in order to do this, she must be trapped in a quite shocking manner, using Sébastien, who wouldn't even know what terrible role he was playing... I'm struggling to believe this and would be grateful if you would reassure me."

"If you are going to adopt that tone of voice, Doctor, I shall be obliged to do likewise!"

The mayor spoke very drily:

"I have indeed written to the pound... which is to say, to the dog's legitimate owners. You do your job, Doctor – I will do mine!"

"How come you never mentioned any of this to me?"

The doctor towered over the mayor, who was able nevertheless to reply with authority:

"We discussed it at length at the municipal council – I thought you knew about it..."

Séraphie, not knowing where to put herself with these two men as they confronted one another, rubbed her hands on her apron, which she had not even thought of removing. She tried her luck:

"At any rate, Doctor, I can assure you that no one knows anything about this up at the house... I advised the village not to mention it in front of Angelina or Jean! As for the boy or his grandfather, we never see them..."

"One thing is certain," continued the mayor, "I have just received a reply from the pound: it's very positive. They will be sending their staff to recapture the animal, and the boy will receive a reward – a tidy sum which will, I imagine, be a pleasant surprise up at the house."

Guillaume slammed the door behind him. He had not waited for the master of the house to show him out. At the thought of this letter which had already been sent to the pound, such rage burned within him that he felt his fists clench.

Naturally enough, since he followed the path almost without realizing it, he was heading towards the house. At the turning, however, he stopped, retraced his steps and veered off to the right. He would go to see old Tonelli; he had just enough time before the start of his surgery. As for seeing Angelina or César, it was impossible: how could he control his anger and not say anything to them? Before speaking out, he needed to think in solitude. He wanted to regain his composure.

He took the least direct, and the least frequented path that follows the sinuous course of the Gordolasque. The snow had been partly swept aside by a sledge: Georges, no doubt, carting wood. Guillaume walked rapidly and nervously.

He soon found himself at the creek where he had built the mill with Sébastien: the little wheel turned proudly.

"I hope no one damages it," Guillaume thought.

At the same time, he thought what a shock it would be for that little child if he happened to learn what was being planned in the village. He had to protect him, to try to sort everything out. What kind of world would it be, Guillaume wondered, if a man, with all his strength and tenderness, was unable to defend a soul that was still so fragile!

He loved Sébastien as he would have loved a child of his own. Or perhaps he loved him because of his great love for Angelina? Of course not. Thinking about it, Guillaume was able to admit to himself that his affection for Sébastien was entirely separate from any other feelings, however strong.

With his foot, he pushed away a branch that the current was driving towards the mill. The branch drifted away, caught by the current; another one took its place. Guillaume took off his mittens and began constructing a dyke that would protect the fragile structure from all the debris carried by the Gordolasque.

The work was nearly finished when he heard a noise that reminded him of a forge's bellows. It was followed by a stifled laugh that Guillaume recognized immediately. He looked up: the boy was leaning against the big dog, both of them balancing on a steep rock above the water on the other side of the mountain stream.

"Sébastien! You little tearaway! Don't lean forward… I'm going to help you down!"

However, in order to help him, he had to make a risky manoeuvre: balancing on a large stone in the middle of the water, stretching out his arm… Sébastien's laugh became extremely annoying.

"You're the one who's going to fall! Look at me! I'm much safer than you."

Guillaume had to admit it: the child was pressing with all his strength on the body of the dog, and she, braced on her four enormous legs, seemed as solid on the sharply sloping rock face as if she were standing on a flat surface. Guillaume admired her with a connoisseur's eye:

"She's magnificent," he said.

The smile Sébastien gave him would have melted an ogre's heart: a mixture of tender pride and candour made his eyes shine. Guillaume noticed that the child and the dog had the same golden gaze, and Sébastien's long dark eyelashes emphasized the resemblance: the bitch's eyelids were likewise painted with two black lines. It was the first time he had noticed it. She was even more beautiful than he had imagined. She did not seem wild.

"Sébastien, do you think if I crossed over she would let me come near?"

His cheeks were pink already, but the blaze of pride made them scarlet.

"I think so, if I ask her to."

"Well then, ask her."

Guillaume had that direct way of speaking that pleases children and soothes animals. Sébastien returned his friendship; in truth, it was a friendship of humans. Would he have the same power over Belle?

She growled when Guillaume set foot on the opposite bank. He extended a friendly hand. Her head jerked back. Guillaume's hand did not move, and Belle, slowly, came and sniffed that hand... which slipped into her fur! That scratching behind her ear was nice! The hand moved: two solid taps on the cheeks followed by a firm and calm voice: "Easy, Belle! There's a good dog! Beautiful girl!"

This ended with a good stroke down her back that cemented their lasting friendship.

Slowly, Belle was becoming a dog again. Sébastien was proud of it:

"You see! They won't be able to say she's vicious! You'll tell them, yes?"

Guillaume nodded. It was better not to broach that subject.

"Have you eaten, Sébastien?"

He had to confess the truth: because he had dashed out of the house when Angelina had opened the door, he was without his snack-filled shoulder bag today.

Guillaume adopted a stern tone:

"Angelina must be very worried. That was wrong of you. Come with me – I'll drop you off when I pass by the house."

Sébastien, however, shook his head: Belle was accustomed to staying with him until sunset. If he left her now, she would think she had been abandoned and – who knows? – everything gained would be lost, she would go feral again!

Guillaume removed a bar of chocolate from his pocket. He always brought a supply with him on his mountain hikes, which sometimes took longer than expected. Sébastien cast a sideways glance at the chocolate. It was his favourite: hazelnut. He said so. It was this frankness of a little savage, one incapable of hiding his pleasure, which enchanted Guillaume:

"All the better," he said, and handed it over.

"All for me?"

"And for Belle."

"What about you?"

Guillaume smiled:

"Me? I eat lunch like most people! Do you promise to come home a little earlier than usual?"

"Yes," Sébastien agreed, "I'll come home as soon as it starts getting dark. Because of Angelina. And because Belle has to eat her lard. You know..." he added confidingly, "I don't think she goes hunting any more – she prefers the soup Angelina makes for her!

Every evening I put it down at the bottom of the steps, and in the morning there's nothing left. Before, she used to come close, but she didn't touch the soup!"

Guillaume rested his hand on the boy's shoulder. "How much longer," he wondered, "will she get the chance to eat this soup that she prefers to hunting?" He squeezed more tightly the little shoulder that felt so fragile in his adult hands.

"You promise, Sébastien, all right? You'll be home at nightfall – I can tell Angelina?"

"Yes, I promise."

Guillaume watched him depart, so confident and so brave. The big dog went ahead of him and turned every so often to give a short bark, as if to encourage him. Then she walked on, and he, placing his feet in the large footprints, followed her in the bright pearly light that drowned the distances where the almost twin summits of the Baou and the Demoiselle stood tall.

Back at the house, Angelina had not calmed down. Indeed, her anger had overtaken her anxiety, and it was reasonable to imagine that, had Sébastien come home when she was working out her rage in needlessly cleaning a meticulous house, his running-away would have left him with painful memories!

However, Guillaume had come to visit. The doctor's presence had a strange power over Angelina:

her usual liveliness, which was considerable, turned into happy tranquillity. It was as if a rose-coloured veil stretched miraculously between herself and reality. Now the same phenomenon occurred to Guillaume as soon as he was in sight of the house: concerns and worries all vanished, and it was with a joyful heart that he whistled the same, unchanging tune that matched his state of mind.

Angelina's trained ear heard it. At once, the old walls of the house witnessed a frantic dance of buckets, rags and brooms as they magically disappeared.

Smiling, with her hair done up, Angelina found herself sitting beside the fire – which burned more joyously – and even the basket willow softened in her hands of its own accord. At first sight, this seemed like magic, but do not be mistaken: these are merely the everyday miracles of love!

Love, however, is not only a crafty and nimble magician; it is also tenderness and solemnity.

"I came up to reassure you, Angelina. I've seen Sébastien. The big dog is with him. You don't have to worry – with her, he's in no danger."

She looked up at him happily.

"You're like Grandfather. He thinks Sébastien is well looked after too, that she would protect him even better than he can!"

He sat facing her and stretched his hands towards the fire. How deeply he loved the simple warmth of this home. Since childhood, he had preferred it to his own. He could not destroy this tranquillity. He could say nothing of what he had learnt from the mayor. For if Angelina knew, there was a danger she would let something slip in front of Sébastien. That, Guillaume wanted to avoid more anything. Who could predict how the child would react when he learnt that the letter sent to the pound threatened to deprive him of Belle? Guillaume might talk to César about it. Yes... to César. Between them, they would try to prepare Sébastien.

The clock with the copper pendulum rang once.

"Don't you find it strange," said Angelina, "the way that animal has let Sébastien get close to it?"

"Not strange," replied Guillaume, "marvellous. When you see them, you let yourself go, you imagine things that, rationally speaking, would be unbelievable."

The pendulum counted out the moments that passed between them, as it had counted out life in the house for generations. As a boy, Guillaume had learnt from César how to handle the weight in order to rewind the mechanism, and now it was Sébastien's turn.

"You see, Angelina, your grandfather's so experienced that his judgement is unfailing. It comes from the fact that he never sees events from the outside, as other men do. He grasps their inner essence, with dignity and kindness. That's why he understands the true meaning of things better than we do. I realized today why we must not treat Sébastien's feelings lightly. He's more fragile, more sensitive and vulnerable than we are. It would be serious – very serious even – to deceive him."

"But," said Angelina, "you know very well that we give him his freedom. He goes and joins that animal wherever she waits for him. To leave the two of them alone, Grandfather no longer goes hunting towards the Baou… I have to admit, this morning…"

Angelina shook her head:

"I ask you! In that fog!"

She stopped herself. A little bitterness crept into her voice when she continued:

"I sometimes wonder if he doesn't love that animal more than us."

"And if that were so? Mustn't you love him for himself and not for you? He's one of those people who needs a passion… He's secretive! He lives in an invisible world that separates him from us, he watches us living without truly sharing our life. He locks himself away in his crystal ball… More than anything, we mustn't shatter that fragile refuge – not when we're dealing with a spirit as fierce as Sébastien's."

As he spoke he watched the flames, and a warm glow flickered across his sensitive face. When they were alone and he spoke to her like this, it was as if a mist parted for Angelina, revealing the true and hidden nature of things. He talked, and she understood everything with ease, wondering that all of this had remained hidden from her for so long.

When he got up to leave, she felt a tearing in the depth of her being – a wound that would heal when, once again, he was physically present beside her.

She thought that he was right and César too; that it would be wrong to prevent Sébastien from running about the mountain with the big white dog, because he needed Belle, as she herself needed Guillaume. Moreover, she knew well that if she no longer had Guillaume, she could die of it, like a plant deprived of water.

On his way back down to the village, Guillaume made up his mind: he too would write to the owner of the pound. As soon as he got home. He would explain the situation to him – man to man – and would ask him to settle on a price for Belle's purchase. Then, he would go to see the notary. He had to find a way of raising enough money. That was yet another problem!

Guillaume began to whistle once more. He shoved his hands into the pockets of his fur-lined jacket. Now that he had made up his mind, he no longer wanted to think about anything... anything other than Angelina and that voice, somewhat shy and very gentle, with which she had asked him:

"Will you come and spend Christmas Eve with us, Doctor? As every year?"

He had said "yes", of course, so long as no one came to fetch him in an emergency to see a patient or deliver a baby. He thought about the enormous box of tinsel and Christmas decorations that he had acquired, buying up Victorine's shop, and that he would bring that very evening to the great joy of Sébastien, Jean, César and... Angelina.

6

At the Amado café, card games were in full swing and the mulled wine was lifting spirits when Moulin junior arrived.

The room was full of men who, having finished work, had come to chat a bit and see friends before going home to spend Christmas Eve with their families. Jean never came, because César forbade it: "You're only seventeen, you can't go to the café," he said. However, Gabriel and François were there – two of his fellow workers on the EDF site – who liked him and worked subtly to protect his innocence, at work and elsewhere.

It had been snowing since nightfall. This was not a long time, but already a pristine layer had transformed the village. People walked on muffled softness, and the quiet took on a peculiar significance. Moulin junior brought all of this in as soon as he opened the door. He was a timid young man, who reminded people of a hare. He came in very proudly, however, thinking he was bringing important news:

"The mayor's had an answer from the pound!"

"Thank you," said his father, who, losing at cards with François, was more furious than ever. "We've already discussed it at the council meeting. From which we have just emerged, for your information. So as news goes, you could have come up with something better."

"Yes," resumed Moulin junior, "but the people from the pound have just telephoned to say that they will be here tomorrow. I just met Madame Séraphie – she's the one who told me."

This time, people were ready to listen, and a good number of men turned towards him with looks of surprise on their faces.

"Trump and trump again!" cried Hippolyte, who added in an infinitely more moderate tone:

"On Christmas Day – what an idea! What does the mayor think about that?"

"He said that, in its way, it's a distraction," declared Moulin junior, "and as there are not many of those round here, especially at Christmas, he agreed."

After this, he went quiet, and did not reopen his mouth to speak all evening.

"I wonder what César will think of it," grumbled Hippolyte.

"And the boy," asked the owner's wife, "little Sébastien? Would he agree to it?"

"Are you stupid or what?"

This was Gabriel, venting his outrage. He was dealing cards. In fact, he was tossing them down, such was his fury at the cruel twist of fate against the house on the mountain. The owner's wife, however, was no less furious, and quite determined to have her revenge:

"If I were as ill-mannered as you, I'd say you were nothing but a lout!"

She turned her back to him ostentatiously and placed a tankard on the table opposite.

"But I'd prefer to tell you something else!"

Moulin junior opened his eyes wide, not daring to involve himself too much in the conversation of his elders, and it was Hippolyte who asked:

"Are we still talking about the dog, or the boy?"

"In a sense…"

The owner's wife was eking out her advantage:

"Félix… You know Félix?"

Everyone nodded at much the same time as Hippolyte.

"Well, Félix is going to get his land at last!"

"What land?"

"The land that belongs to the doctor... Saint-Jacques, with the cottage."

"Don't tell me the doctor's selling him that land! With the cottage too!"

"Eh, well, I am saying it, because I happen to know."

Sure enough, it was true! Meanwhile, Séraphie, as she prepared turkey with chestnuts for the evening feast, was commenting on news that flabbergasted the mayor:

"Are you sure about this, Séraphie?"

"I've just told you, the little typist – Rosine, you know – saw them with the notary. Félix and the doctor! They were signing."

"But why is the doctor selling Saint-Jacques?"

Why? Because Félix was in a hurry to establish himself on some land, and Guillaume had found a way of amassing a substantial sum of ready money with which to buy Belle! It was that simple. Except, at present, he was the only one who knew it.

It snowed all night. Then came Christmas Day. The snow had stopped. The air was cold and dry. A fine day. César had gone out on the mountain before first light. The previous evening he had located the tracks of a white fox. This morning, he was looking for its den. When he found it, he would bring Sébastien, and together they would wait to catch a glimpse of the pretty little animal. It was old César's Christmas present, and he knew that Sébastien would appreciate it.

Jean had gone out a little later. As every Christmas morning for years, he was the one who brought the household's good wishes for happiness and peace to the village.

Everyone was getting ready for the celebrations; everyone felt a warm glow of joy and wellbeing.

When Sébastien woke up, he saw the Christmas tree in front of the chimney and Angelina hanging up brilliant baubles of every colour. They chimed softly as they knocked together in her hands. Sébastien waited a long time, pretending to be asleep. The young woman started wrapping her masterpiece, the tinsel garland, around the tree. Sébastien yawned.

"It's pretty," he said.

Angelina turned her beaming face towards him:

"Are you not asleep, you naughty boy? I haven't finished! I was hoping to surprise you!"

"It's still a surprise. It's already very pretty!"

He jumped out of bed and washed as quickly as he could. Angelina was far too busy this morning to notice. As every day, Sébastien joined Belle, who was waiting for him, this time very close to the house. Angelina scarcely saw her hidden behind a great block of stone adjoining the shed.

She gestured towards Sébastien, not unkindly:

"You're not staying outside all day today, Sébastien! I'm expecting you for lunch. If you only knew what lovely things we're having! Happy Christmas, dear Sébastien, and to Belle too!"

In the distance, Sébastien burst out laughing:

"Thank you from her! Happy Christmas!"

Angelina quickly shut the door to keep in the warmth.

Together, the big dog and the child walked towards the spruce wood that follows the Gordolasque.

The snow was so thick this morning that César, seeing them walk along the ridge above the house, watched Sébastien from a distance. He was careful not to call out or reveal himself. He marvelled and felt more confident than ever: never before had he encountered a dog so endowed with good instincts. Belle only allowed the child to run after she had sniffed the snow and tamped it down, and the one time Sébastien had wandered from the path thus marked out for him, she had pushed him back with her powerful muzzle. Treating this as a game, he tried to escape: she caught up with him, always bringing him back to where she knew the going was safe. César, who had seen so many dogs, sheepdogs and hunting dogs, who knew those great rescue animals, St Bernards, remained astonished and full of admiration.

Having completed her task, Angelina stood back a little to consider her achievement. Yes, she was quite proud of her tree! Now she was going to go down to the village and pay her visit to the cemetery.

The mule Paquita was quickly saddled and, with her red pompons and her three little bells ringing out, she carried Angelina towards the valley.

The cemetery of Saint-Martin, located on the side of the mountain above the village, is one of the most poetic and tranquil places imaginable. On the morning of every feast day, Angelina went to spend some time there. These visits felt natural to her: her parents were resting there, united in death as they had been in their short life together, and nearby lay that woman whom they could not have known, about whom nothing was known except that she had been Sébastien's mother. It was Angelina's task to include them in the joys and worries of the household. Today, her dextrous fingers decorated a Christmas tree just like the one she had prepared at the house. She sang softly as she worked, quite without sorrow. She felt great tenderness.

"It's a nice idea, Angelina – that tinsel, those red baubles…"

She turned abruptly, like a startled doe.

"Oh! Doctor… Luckily I recognize your voice, or you'd have frightened me."

She finished her delicate work and added:

"At this time of year, there are only artificial flowers, and I don't like them. I'd rather they have a Christmas tree like the rest of us. You still think it's pretty, don't you?"

Guillaume concurred enthusiastically:

"It's pretty like everything you do. Do you know, I have never seen a table as beautifully decorated as yours at the house last night? It looked even better than last year's."

She blushed at the compliment, also perhaps with emotion. She saw him practically every day, yet here, their solitude seemed more intimate and more solemn. Guillaume's voice sounded more serious than usual:

"I was on my way back from seeing old Tonelli. I noticed your mule first and then… I saw you."

She stood motionless, her eyes fixed on the bluish horizon where the snowy peaks rose, distinct and pure in the freezing air. She could not speak; it was as if a hand were squeezing her throat.

"Angelina…"

The grip around her throat loosened. She felt that Guillaume must be able to hear the beating of her heart.

"Angelina, what I have to tell you…"

He made no move, not even a gesture to take hold of her hand. He too stared at the blue horizon. He said her name again:

"Angelina…"

Then, very simply, he added:

"Will you marry me?"

Now their eyes met, youthful and sombre, full of the joy that was ready to burst out behind their emotion at this moment, a moment that they would remember until the end of their lives, the moment when, almost without speaking, they declared their love for one another. They seemed almost weighed down by it.

"Angelina…"

"Guillaume…"

Very softly, frightened a little by so much happiness, she added:

"I've always loved you… as far back as I can remember."

Jean had called on the mayor, the priest, the headmaster and many others. He was leaving the doctor's house, having failed to find him, but Célestine had accepted his good wishes and offered her own.

It was Gabriel, however, who first told him about the mayor's letter, about the pound's reply and the arrival of specialist personnel that very afternoon.

"So what if it is a daft thing to do? I should probably have kept quiet, but I thought if was shameful to let all those people go up to the Baou without you knowing what they're planning to do there… What will your grandfather say about it?"

Jean, floored by the news, did not react.

"And the kid?" Gabriel continued. "What should we do?"

This was exactly what Jean was thinking, and he could see no solution.

"Why don't you talk to Doctor Guillaume about it?"

"I'll discuss it first with my grandfather. I doubt he knows about it… As if! There'd have been some scene in the village, if he'd known such a thing."

"He'll have to warn the boy… He's the only one who can do it, don't you think?"

César, however, was not yet home, and Jean was only able to talk to his sister. They arrived at the same time from the village – him on foot, her on her mule, her heart full of intense joy. Now this news!

"What will Sébastien do?"

At once, she added:

"Luckily, he's on the mountain. So is Grandfather. They'll come back for lunch and we'll see them both... If would be terrible if the little one learnt all this from somebody else."

"If only we'd known sooner... We might have been able to do something."

"It wouldn't have made any difference."

Instinctively, Angelina repeated the word that the doctor had already used:

"It's disgraceful."

Jean was silent. He knew very well that, at this point, even César could do nothing.

"Since it's Christmas," said Angelina, "couldn't they let him have his happiness?"

Jean nodded. Nobody in the village had thought how to handle the boy on this holiday, which that, more than any other, is for children. Nobody, not even Gabriel. Because nobody, except perhaps Guillaume and César, truly understood that Sébastien loved Belle with an extraordinary love that was stronger than life itself.

Without realizing it, brother and sister looked at the great white expanse of snow that spread its indifferent softness all the way to the impassive summits. Suddenly the weather had turned notably milder. It was almost warm. A spring warmth.

"Can you feel it...? It's the thaw," said Jean.

Angelina's mind was elsewhere: already, she was suffering for Sébastien.

"We'll keep him in this afternoon and this evening… We're sure to find a reason. And later on, Grandfather will explain to him…'

"Or he could go with him onto the mountain, and tell him there."

Angelina bowed her head. She knew perfectly well that either way, eventually, the heartbreak would be such that Sébastien's fragile spirits would never recover.

However, the ways of God are mysterious, and it was Georges who told Sébastien. The child was walking through the spruce wood and the man was coming back with his horse, dragging a log through the snow – a huge tree trunk stripped of its bark, which dragged from left to right along the path, creating banks on either side. The man was furious at having to work on Christmas Day, but he was behind on his delivery to the sawmill and had to make up lost time.

Belle, with her ears cocked, had heard him coming well before Sébastien noticed the sound of the horse's little bells and the clanking of the chains that dragged the tree. She had fled with one bound. Motionless, on the edge of the wood, she waited for Sébastien to be alone again before rejoining him.

"Where's your beast?" asked Georges.

Sébastien gestured proudly with his head to indicate the vastness of the mountain behind him.

"You're in luck! She'll fetch a tidy sum for you when they catch her."

Perhaps he was not a bad man, and maybe he was fooled by Sébastien's attitude, thinking him indifferent: with his head bowed, he was digging at the snow with the toe of his little boot.

"There's no shortage of dogs in the world," continued Georges when Sébastien gave no reply.

The child lifted his head. He always had that proud look that came naturally to him and that people mistook for haughtiness.

"No one can catch Belle... No one!"

This was all he could think of to say, the only words that came to him, his feeble defence! And he stamped his foot in the snow.

"No one... No one can catch her."

The man roared with laughter.

"That's what you think! No one, you say. Well, you'll see for yourself, and soon, too... Heave-ho, Carcass!"

Sébastien could still hear him when he lost sight of him, hidden by a bend in the Gordolasque. Then he ran towards the house, his only refuge. César! He had to find César. César would tell him if this was true.

The shortest route was the one through the wood. He ran, a little figure shadowed by the trees that soared straight up to block out the daylight. On the ground, the fragrant layer of dead needles was covered up with snow; so were rocks and fallen branches. Twice he fell and got up again. He had not hurt himself. He ran on. Tiredness, however, robbed him of his agility and, in his third fall, he injured himself. His head struck the foot of one of the tall trees hard.

This was where Belle found him.

In the village, Gabriel and François, somewhat intimidated by the gleaming parquet floor and the polished furniture, walked into Doctor Guillaume's house.

François was the one who had thought of approaching the doctor, but it was Gabriel who spoke:

"I've already told Jean everything, but he's very young – who knows if he'll be able to explain, and you know what César's like, the rages he can fly into! Whereas you, Doctor… Just think! There isn't a moment to lose – they'll be here soon to catch the animal."

Guillaume was pale, containing his outrage. Nonetheless, fury was mounting inside him.

"Since they dare take away a child's happiness and reason for being on Christmas Day, they shall have me to answer to."

Gabriel smiled broadly, and a flicker of joy passed across François's face.

"That's what we were hoping," said Gabriel. "It's just that, you see, we don't have your gift with words! As for him" – he pointed at François – "he was all for fetching his gun and joining the old man on the mountain."

Guillaume gave his warm, comforting laugh.

"We'll try to sort things out some other way... Thank you for coming to let me know."

In the event, he was prevented from reaching the house by the loud and desperate barking that he heard the moment he reached the first bend in the track. Belle was calling for help. Guillaume changed course towards this cry.

She called out several times to guide the doctor. When he saw her, she stood out white against the sombre line of trees. She ran ahead of him and entered the dark wood. He followed her tracks all the way to the little slumped body that lay, curled up in a ball, at the foot of one of the straight and mighty tree trunks. The child was sobbing quietly – a poor little rag, drained of strength. Next to him, Guillaume picked up the handkerchief with which Sébastien had mopped up the blood that was seeping from his forehead. It was nothing serious, but Guillaume seized the opportunity, the pretext, to keep the child at his house. Without Sébastien, Belle would be impossible to catch, and he, for his part, would be freer to say what he had to say to everyone if he knew that the child was safe. Yes, the best thing to do was to take him home, to the village.

Sébastien struggled, refusing to be taken away:

"Belle... They'll catch her, they'll kill her..."

With that, he burst into tears again. Guillaume hesitated: should he tell Sébastien that he was trying to buy Belle? He was almost sure to get her but, in the meantime, those men they were expecting would try to capture Belle, Sébastien might hear about it and lose hope... So he promised quietly:

"They will not kill her. I'm here to protect her. Do you believe me, Sébastien?"

He stopped for a brief moment to show him the big dog, motionless behind them. She watched them go down towards the village. All of a sudden, she turned away, and Sébastien saw her escaping towards the Baou. Only then, with his mind at ease, did he allow himself to be carried.

He let himself be bandaged up, his impassive little face closed in thought. He stared into space.

Passively, he drank the infusion prescribed by the doctor. He offered no resistance when Célestine laid him down on the living-room divan. Then he closed his eyes. Guillaume bent towards him:

"I'm going to the house to tell César and Angelina that you're with me. Sleep, my little savage… Sleep."

Sébastien did not even open his eyes.

"He'll sleep," said Guillaume. "You look after him, Célestine. Keep him here: he must not go out. It won't seem like it tomorrow, but he has to have peace and quiet…"

No sooner was the door closed than Célestine gave vent to her temper: she thought about the Christmas meal she had worked so hard to prepare and the trouble she had put herself to. Very likely, it would have to wait! The doctor would come back late… or not at all, as sometimes happened when he had to stay with one of his patients. Only, this time he would not have that excuse: he was going up to the house… to see Angelina! Any pretext would do!

Célestine heaved a heavy sigh and went to half-open the window. The tall figure of the doctor was departing with broad strides. He was already far away. She stood there for a moment, breathing in the air. She too noticed how mild the weather had turned.

"It's the thaw," she said.

Exactly as Angelina and Jean had remarked a little earlier, and Guillaume noted as he went up the mountain, taking off his hat and scarf and unbuttoning his jacket. As César thought when, on his way back to the house, he noticed Guillaume approaching.

The old man repeated it, only this time with a sort of worried prescience when Guillaume had explained everything to them.

César had opened the door some time ago. Now, standing on the threshold, he smelt the warmth of the air, he watched the great black cloud surmounting the Baou, rising up, growing until it filled the sky. He muttered simply:

"It looks like the mountain's about to get angry."

In the doctor's living room, Célestine's head nodded gently from right to left, and Sébastien was watching her. Previously, it had been the other way round: Célestine had been tenderly watching the boy's face, the enchanted smile on his lips and the shadow of his long lashes cast on cheeks that had regained their rosiness. Sébastien was smiling, for, in the obstinate silence with which he opposed all this comfort around him, he had made up his mind.

He had to save Belle, and he was all alone to do it. He had no confidence in anyone else: no one had warned him. They said they loved the big dog… César, Angelina, the doctor, Jean too – but how could they? No, Sébastien knew what he had to do. Perhaps it was not entirely clear in his six-year-old mind, but he was sure of one thing: that he would lead her far away, to a place where men would never come looking for her.

Now, Célestine was asleep, she was even snoring a little, and Sébastien, fully dressed apart from his boots, tried to decide whether to wait a little longer or to leave at once.

A loud snore from Célestine made up his mind. He got up, went to her, waved a hand under her nose, hesitated for an instant and finally made a frightful grimace. No reaction. Célestine was in the Land of Nod.

He crossed the garden, heading not for the road, of course, but towards the little door that opened onto the footpath. It was easy, and Sébastien escaped unnoticed from the village, conjured away by that strange magician, Destiny.

At first, he ran very fast. Soon, however, the deep snow brought him back to the long, slow rhythm of the mountain. He crossed the Gordolasque on the tree trunk that had withstood so many springs. The watermill built by the doctor was still spinning in its little creek. Sébastien turned away: he was in too much of a hurry. Besides, his bet was no longer valid since he would never again go down to the house, or the village... He would never go to school. He was going to live up there, with Belle! He called out to her:

"Belle!"

In the quiet, his shout travelled the whole length of the mountain. He had reached the level of the fork, but on the other side of the Grand Défilé, where the moraine breaks up and forms a furrow parallel with the Défilé, under the rocky ridge of the Pas-du-Loup.

"Belle!"

She came towards him slowly, her head bowed. Anyway, there she was. She gave a hoarse whimper and, strangely, the plume of her tail would not stop beating. Still she kept her head lowered. He wanted to lead her away, and she walked at his side. Or rather, she crept along, as if she were ill.

"What's the matter? What do you want?"

They started to climb again; it was so mild that Sébastien threw away his scarf. Ahead of them lay the Grand Défilé, the corridor of doom, and above them, the southern flank of the Baou: rotten stone and crests too steep for snow to cling to for long. Yet so much snow had fallen in the last few days that this side of the Baou was entirely white, with large dark surfaces between the ridges.

Laughing with joy, his coat wide open, he set off down the rocky corridor. Belle whimpered and lay down. He went back to her.

"What's the matter, Belle, are you hurt?"

He stroked the whole of her body with his hands: she let him do so while continuing to whine, a hoarse whimper that Sébastien did not recognize. He felt furious all of a sudden:

"No one comes this way... Don't you understand? That's why we have to go into the Grand Défilé! Because they're frightened. All of them. If only you could understand! Wait! I know you'll follow me."

He left her there, and went on down the avalanche corridor. The dog stood up. She whimpered but followed him. And because she went so slowly, he tied his belt around her:

"You're going to follow me, even if you don't like it. And quickly. We have to hide before they see us."

Really, the weather was close, it was so tiring having to pull Belle, and he still had a bit of a headache. He threw away his hat. Suddenly, without warning, Belle braced herself on her four legs, refusing to go any farther. This was so abrupt that Sébastien fell over. Trembling all over, she remained stock-still.

"What's the matter with you?"

Above his head, there was a rushing sound: a gust of wind. Yet the air around him remained motionless and heavy. He looked up towards the Baou: the sky was turning a dark grey and there, above the great neckline of the rock wall, he saw the Baou with its vertical crests covered in fresh snow. It appeared to be moving…

With one bound, Belle was at his side. She had stopped whimpering and was using all of her regained strength to push Sébastien with her nose and flank. He, all but carried along, clung to the thick fur of her neck. She pushed him, dragged him towards a corner where the wall had eroded at the base. She jostled him until he almost fell into a sort of little cave sheltered by the great wall. Sébastien was frightened. Frightened of the sky, frightened of the Baou, frightened of Belle who would not let go of him, forcing him to walk, to crouch down, so small against these mighty forces. When he was up against the rock, at the far end of the cave, she all but lay on top of him.

It began with a cloud of powdery snow, and the whole mountain growling. Sébastien covered his face with his arms; he screamed:

"Belle!"

And, wrapping his arms about the dog's neck, he hid his face in her fur. She, braced on her four legs, put all of her strength into trapping him against the rock whose overhang protected him, and into covering his body. This was when she gave the long, terrible howl that they heard at the house. The great cry of horror at the avalanche.

Belle's cry, repeated and amplified by the mountain echo, was heard by Célestine too, at the very moment she met Michel Boudu on his way back from the municipal ski jump. She had left the doctor's house panic-stricken by Sébastien's disappearance, and was going up to the house to warn the doctor, to warn them all, that Sébastien had escaped! Where to? Who could tell with him? It was for this reason that she was running as she had never run before, since deep down she was not confident that she would find the boy in the house on the mountain.

"Listen, Michel… Go to César – see if Sébastien has come home!"

"Sébastien?" interrupted Michel. "But I saw him… He was heading for the Pas-du-Loup."

"Holy Mother! Run, quick… You tell them. I'll follow."

They were all on the threshold of the house. César had just murmured, "It looks like the mountain's set about get angry," when, through the close and abnormally warm air, the mountain sent them Belle's cry. They all froze.

"It's the dog… It's Belle calling for help!"

Angelina stifled a cry:

"My God!"

But her voice was lost in the low and horrifyingly powerful rumble that was invading the mountain…

The avalanche.

It was at this moment that they noticed Michel Boudu. He was calling out to them from the bend, but in the midst of that deadly great growl they could not hear him. He had to come up very close before they were able to listen.

"Madame Célestine sent me… Sébastien is on the mountain – he got away. She wants to know if he has come home… I saw him going up towards the Pas-du-Loup…"

Poor Michel was spluttering; what he had just said reached the others alongside the gigantic rumble of the avalanche. This went on for a few more seconds, and then silence regained possession of the world as if nothing had happened, as if Belle had not cried out, as if the mountain had not moved.

Guillaume was the first to come back to his senses. His hand gripped the boy's shoulder hard enough to hurt him, but finally he spoke and his orders came out:

"Go down as fast as you can... Bring back men. Everyone you can find. With shovels. Tell them Sébastien is on the mountain and we have to save him..."

How he ran, poor Michel! He had so often chanted "Sébastien... gypsy!" at the little one, and now, if he had wings – oh, he would have flown to the village, crying out, "Sébastien's on the mountain... Sébastien's on the mountain..."

Up there, Guillaume was running towards the Baou. He had sent Jean to the customs post to alert the officers. César had attempted to persuade Angelina:

"It will be hard enough for the men – wait here."

Wait! She would have gone insane! No, she was the one who had held him in her arms, six years ago, and now, if he had to be carried one final time into their home, she would not let it be in anyone's arms but her own. There was nothing more for César to say. She went with him.

They all walked towards the Baou, towards its southern flank, since Sébastien had last been seen by Michel near the Pas-du-Loup.

Soon, however, voices are calling out from all corners of the mountain: the customs men, the gendarmes and all the men of the village, all shouting only one name: "Sébastien!" Angelina has caught up with Guillaume. They cry out at intervals and, when their voices cease, silence reclaims the mountain. An inhuman desert. Silence. They walk towards the Grand Défilé, Guillaume having found the scarf and, farther on, the hat. In a line, all scour the great sea of snow from which, here and there, a few monstrous tips of rock emerge.

"It's impossible," says Guillaume suddenly, "it's impossible that the dog, with the instincts of her breed, would not have sensed the avalanche, that she wouldn't have led him to safety."

"She may have tried, but that doesn't mean she succeeded…"

For Angelina has lost all hope. Faced with this depth of snow… No, there is no hope.

Now Guillaume is almost angry:

"Why should she not have succeeded, Angelina? Why? Even if there were only one chance in a thousand… that chance exists! Come on – you need to search on the edge of an avalanche."

And he takes up the call again:

"Hey! What's that?..."

Angelina grabs his arm and grips it:

"Guillaume! I'm going mad! I think I can hear the dog!"

"Belle!" shouts Guillaume.

When his voice gives out and silence resettles, a stifled growl replies.

"On the left," cries Angelina… "She's barking!"

Guillaume has heard it as well. He turns towards the men, waves them over and points them in the right direction.

The men are only searching just in case. They know perfectly well that, under such a thickness of snow, it will not be possible to find anything until the spring… Nonetheless, they follow the doctor.

They catch up with him near an overhanging rock, against which two uprooted spruce trees are leaning with what remains of their branches. Immediately, they leap into action with their shovels and picks, clearing around the rock.

"Stop digging," cries Guillaume.

He knelt down between the tree trunks and the rock face. Digging with his hands, little by little, he uncovered the dog. She did not whimper but, instead of freeing herself, which she could have done, she remained motionless. The breath was audible from her buried muzzle. Guillaume, level with her breast, discovered a foot inside a boot that everyone recognized… They stood there, frozen and so silent that the only sound was of Belle's panting.

"Everyone," ordered Guillaume, "hold up the trees in case they slip."

He was able to slide his hand under the dog and place it above Sébastien's heart. Kneeling beside him, Angelina sobbed quietly. Guillaume righted himself:

"HE'S ALIVE!"

César tried lifting the dog's head to uncover the child's face. Belle freed herself with a growl and resumed the position she had kept since the start of the avalanche: her body protecting Sébastien's and her hot breath warming the face so that the snow could not cover it up. This was how she had saved him. Only Guillaume was able to persuade her to get up. He took off his wool-lined jacket and slipped it carefully under the child. Now he was able to examine him.

Soon, Sébastien opened his eyes. His first cry was: "Belle…'

"She's here," said César. "Nobody's going to hurt her."

Upon which the mayor said what everyone was thinking:

"Oh, no! That's over and done with! You'll have your dog, I promise you that."

Guillaume had lifted Sébastien and was going down, carrying him in his arms, towards the house. Everyone else followed: César, and Jean, who was supporting Angelina, and the others – all of them. Now that fear was gone, tongues loosened; it was as if the whole mountain bristled with voices.

The most extraordinary thing, however, was Belle's attitude. At first, she had kept her distance, she followed the doctor who was carrying Sébastien, but from a way off and to the side. Then, all of a sudden, she caught up with him. And it was she who led the way to the house... She was the first to climb the steps. And there she waited, sitting motionless beneath the "sign" as it turned in the evening breeze.

Over towards the Baou, all was quiet, as if the mountain had never had its moment of fury, as if it were falling asleep, indifferent to all the noise that it had occasioned. And Belle looked at it. The Beast turned away from its immense solitudes; rediscovering the founding act of her distant ancestor, she consented to live amongst people.

Everyone from the village departed. They spoke little on the way down. Even so, the mayor met Gabriel's eye. Then he said:

"This is one Christmas we won't forget!"

The men from the dog pound arrived in Saint-Martin shortly after the avalanche. They were quite poorly received. People explained very succinctly what remained for them to do, which was to go away again!

Then, the day after New Year's Day, the reply to the doctor's letter arrived: Belle was for sale, and the owner of the pound sought a hefty price for her. Belle for sale! How absurd was that? Belle was not for sale: Belle had chosen Sébastien.

Nonetheless, Guillaume bought her. But he kept it a secret, and no one knew a thing about it.

Henceforth, the house on the mountain was full of Belle's magnificent presence. She slept in front of the hearth, large and, it seemed, as calm as a bearskin. But all it took was a visitor for her eye to light up and her ears to rise. When Sébastien went down to the village for Saturday market, he took her with him. People were quiet as he passed, and nobody called him "the gypsy" any more.

Then came the first buds of spring. With his satchel on his shoulder, Sébastien took the path to school, for the doctor's mill was still spinning, and a promise is a promise.

It was around this time that Angelina and Guillaume were married, to the great joy of everybody and the despair of Célestine, who would no longer reign alone over the doctor's waxed parquet floors and his gleaming furniture.

What else can I tell you?... That if there is happiness in the world, it belonged to Belle and Sébastien.

– December 1964

Glossary

appropriate   To take something.

apse   A semicircular recess in a church.

arabesque   An ornamental Islamic pattern.

arduous   Very difficult and tiring.

baou   French name – a hill with a flat top.

Belle   From the French for "beautiful".

bitch   A female dog.

candour   Truthfulness; honesty.

chasm   A deep hole.

cirque   A semicircular hollow in a glacier.

complicity   Involvement in immoral activities with someone else.

compress   A pad used to stop bleeding.

conciliatory   Trying to reconcile.

connoisseur   An expert on a given subject.

coomb   A small valley or hollow on the side of a hill or mountain.

Dahu   A mythical mountain animal with short legs on one side for walking on steep mountain sides.

domestication   The process of taming an animal.

downed tools   Stopped working.

EDF	Électricité de France, the main electricity supplier in France.
eking out	Making something last.
entrenched	Deeply seated.
ewe	A female sheep.
facetiously	Light-heartedly mocking.
feral	Wild.
gambol	Playful running.
game	A hunted animal.
garrotte	Strangle someone with wire.
gendarmerie	The local headquarters of the gendarmes, a French police unit.
gudgeon	A small fish used as bait.
imperturbably	Calmly.
irrefutably	Undeniably.
kinship	Deep bond.
levity	Using humour in a serious situation.
litany	Repeated phrase or song.
litter	A set of newborn animals.
moraine	A mass of rocks which have collected at the bottom of a glacier.
municipal council	The council of a local authority in France.
opened hostilities	Started fighting.
ostentatiously	Purposefully showy.
Paradine Beast	A forgotten legendary monster.
pediment	A feature, triangular in shape, mounted above a door.

pedlar	Salesperson.
perverse	Deliberately acting unreasonably.
pieds et paquets	A Provençal dish made of sheep's feet and stuffed sheep's tripe.
pinnacle	The high point of a mountain.
prescience	Knowing something in advance.
Provençal	Of or relating to Provence.
refuge	A hut in the Alps, built to shelter people from bad weather.
rejoinder	Reply; retort.
ruminations	Deep thoughts or musings.
salivate	To relish the idea of something.
Saut-du-Loup	French for 'The Wolf's Leap'.
sceptical	Untrusting; doubtful.
scree	Steep cliffs covered in loose stones.
scrutinized	Studied; gazed intensely at.
sexton	A church caretaker.
sheepfold	An enclosure for keeping sheep in.
solemnity	Seriousness.
solitude	Being alone; a lonely place.
Tarasque	A legendary monster of Provence, tamed by St Martha.
time immemorial	A time so long ago that nobody can remember it.
vertigo	A fear of heights; causes dizziness.
Victory	An allegorical figure in ancient Greek sculpture.